ISBN 978-1-5276-7295-6
PIBN 10879902

HIGH-WAYS AND BY-WAYS;

OR,

TALES OF THE ROADSIDE,

PICKED UP IN THE FRENCH PROVINCES.

BY

A WALKING GENTLEMAN.

T. C. Grattan

SECOND SERIES.

"I hate the man who can travel from Dan to Beersheba, and says, 'Tis all barren." *Sterne.*

A NEW EDITION.

IN THREE VOLUMES.

VOL. II.

LONDON:
PRINTED FOR HENRY COLBURN,
NEW BURLINGTON-STREET.

1825.

R. B. P.

LONDON:

SHACKELL AND ARROWSMITH, JOHNSON'S-COURT, FLEET-STREET.

THE PRIEST,

AND

THE GARDE-DU-CORPS.

VOL. II.

THE PRIEST,

AND

THE GARDE DU-CORPS.

CHAPTER I.

The reader who has accompanied me thus far, needs not be told that my predilections are not for cities, and may have surmised my aversion towards what are termed in the parlance of war *strong places*. They only who have been "cribbed and cabined" for months together within the walls of a garrison, can fully comprehend the vigorous simplicity of Cowper's obvious, but not the less original phrase—

"God made the country, and man made the town."—

And nothing short of such a situation can

give a true relish for the open walks of nature, where, to use Lord Bacon's words, "the scent of air comes and goes like the warblings of music."

In the ramparted cages to which I allude, every thing is stagnant. All possibility of improvement is excluded, for a boundary is set to moral as well as physical expansion; and an unbroken mediocrity is decreed for generation after generation. The town seems to have sprung, like the children of the fabled mythology, at once from infancy to manhood. A dwarfish precocity has forced the place from its plan to its completion; and it stands a premature pattern of still life and middle age, without the pleasing irregularities of a young establishment, or the touching prognostics of picturesque decay. The inhabitants partake of this prim formality. They are the most regular and least amiable of beings. All the functions of society seem performed by beat of drum. Nothing degenerates or improves. Variety, the brightest charm of life, is unworshipped where the despotism of monotony is bowed down to. Not one sentiment, or impulse, or instinct, seems to revel uncontrouled; and I doubt which calculation is more considered—the quantity of provisions which the population may consume, or the number of mouths which it is expedient to provide for its consumption. All this matter-of-fact slavery is most revolting to one of my rambling turn; and it is rarely that I cross the drawbridge of a garrison town.

One evening, however, during a straggling tour through Flanders, I found myself almost benighted at the gate of one of its strongest fortresses, at that time held by some Prussians, forming part of the army of occupation under the Duke of Wellington's command. I had hoped to pass round the place, and reach a village a couple of leagues further on my route; but I had loitered in pursuit of a scattered covey of birds that had led me a long and fruitless chace across the almost interminable plains

The dusky haze of a September evening forced me to give up the pursuit; and the night was nearly closing in as I recovered the main road, and trudged along, listening to the rustling of the breeze in the standing oats that skirted each side of the paved causeway. The business of the day being over, the peasants of this unlovely region had all closed their huts, and shut their eyes no doubt, upon the joyless world. The desolate bleakness around me made me almost long for darkness, as preferable to the dim monotony of the scene. The distant drums and bugles from the town broke at length on my ear, as they sounded their day dirge to the garrison within; and the wild blast with its rolling accompaniment awoke a train of thoughts of many a former associate, scattered across the surface of the earth or deeply shrined beneath it. Every step I took seemed to rouse a recollection, like the spirit of some departed scene; and I walked on, in imagined communion with the shades of a less material world.

The sounds gradually died away, and I entered the wretched suburb that looked like a dangling excrescence to the place. The houses of this suburb were so miserable that I, though never over-nice, could not reconcile myself to their outside appearance, or venture my foot within; so I walked up to the moat of a little outwork thrown before the place, and, answering the hoarse challenge of a Prussian sentinel, demanded that the bridge might be lowered and I admitted into the town.

It is not necessary to detail the worrying, but perhaps essential, formalities which consumed nearly an hour, before I could take possession of a comfortless bed in the nearest inn. The night passed over as it might; and I rose early, preparing to continue my journey. But the clouds lowered, and the rain poured down, and I was obliged to postpone my departure, and submit to my irksome imprisonment. While I breakfasted and attempted to read or write a little, I heard the well remembered call *for parade*, blown by the bugles and echoed by the drums. There was something vivifying in the sound, which I conjectured to mean more than a mere garrison muster on so wet a morning. I aroused Ranger from his slumber, and proposed a walk, preferring the certainty of a shower without, in search of the meaning of these notes of preparation, to the tedium of a sojourn within. We accordingly sallied out into the street, and soon came to the principal square, where the regular garrison was already in the ranks, and the national guard straggling in. All the authorities of the place were soon collected; and the crowd was made up of an incongruous assemblage of military, civil, and religious distinctions. In answer to my enquiries, I was informed that in honor of some royal reminiscence, a *Te Deum* was about to be chanted in the cathedral church, and all the preliminary arrangements being completed, the procession was quickly formed; and as the town clock struck twelve it began its march. It rained violently; and whether from this cause, or the more probable one of indifference to these sort of things, but few of the town's-people attended; but the train was swelled out by some curious or idle interlopers, among whom myself and Ranger made muster. The foreign part of the warlike train seemed ill at ease under the shower that was tarnishing their lace and accoutrements; the citizen-soldiers looked sulky and tawdry; the town magistrates tripped mincingly across the dirty pavement in their silk stockings and scarfs; the priests alone trudged carelessly through the gutters, their vestments dabbling in the mud, their hats under their arms, their tonsured skulls exposed to the cold and the invidious drops which trickled through their shabby umbrellas.

From the Hotel de Ville whence we started, we were accompanied to church by a band of music, which, with the regular troops, formed in two lines at each side of the open porch. As I looked through the vista made by their ranks,

I saw the massive columns of the church within, standing in dusky solemnity, and forming a lengthened avenue, beyond which I caught a glimpse of the altar, shining far away in gorgeous decoration. Some scattered attendants in white surplices flitted to and fro across its steps; and the vapours of incense, mixed with the duskier clouds exhaled by the gigantic tapers, threw an air of awful mystery over the distant scene.

As I gazed, and already seemed to catch the shadowy inspiration of the place, I was startled —almost shocked indeed—to observe the leading priest preceded up the aisle by four drummers and about a dozen of the national guard, the former rolling their drums, the echoes of which reverberated wildly through the building. To my increasing astonishment and dismay, this advanced party ascended the steps of the altar, and their careless yet measured tramp struck with unholy echoes upon the sacred floor. They ranged themselves at each side, to the total exclusion of their reverend followers, who occupied seats raised in front at some yards distance. Several females were in the church before our arrival, and being all in their fête dresses, decorated with flowers, and generally good looking, they threw a lighter grace upon the otherwise sombre scene. The general and his staff, with the magistracy and some decently attired civilians, came next in order. I was amongst this group, to which succeeded the less respectable looking stragglers, and a few old women of the lower class. Ranger had slipped in unobserved, and crouched nervously between my legs.

The military were ranged down the aisle in triple ranks, with bayonets fixed and shouldered arms, their long plumes waving high above the bare heads of the less privileged spectators. The bustle of their arrangement having subsided and order being obtained, the *Te Deum* commenced. The performers were stationed in the gallery at the farthest extremity of the church, and as the soft pealings of the organ swelled out their opening cadences, the notes seemed to sink into my heart, and calmed for a while the rather ruffled sensations excited by the former parts of the ceremony.

But this quiet tone was soon broken in upon, when the orchestra, vocal and instrumental, chimed forth its dissonant interruption. The performers altogether did not exceed a dozen; and the faint scrapings of some ill-tuned violins, mingled with harsh voices, grated odiously upon my ear, and seemed a mockery of the solemn place. Their discord was at times most seasonably interrupted by the rattling of the indefatigable drummers, who on one occasion rather overdid their parts; for an old priest, whose physiognomy spoke him at once good-natured and irascible, motioned them with violent gestures to desist. But, ludicrously enough, they supposed that the actions of raising his arm, striking his clenched fist against his thigh, stamping his foot, and shaking his head, urged them to increase their labours—and indeed his movements were any thing but *pianissimo*—and the noise was in consequence for a time increased ten-fold. Twice during the ceremony the altar guard presented arms, and went through some other evolutions, which found no imitation from the ranks, formed down the aisle, standing stiff and formal as if on their regular parade.

When the music had ceased, two of the best dressed and best looking of the ladies went round to collect money, and smilingly solicited contributions for their silver plates. Two or three pieces of gold and a few of the larger silver coins rewarded their efforts. I thought myself almost too moderate in my donation, but was quite surpassed in economy by a flashy looking native beside me, decorated with the cross of the legion of honour, and two other orders to boot, who placed a sous on the plate with a significant glance at me, which seemed to say "You are a Greenhorn !"

The procession left the church, forming the same order in which it had advanced. I quitted it at the door—filled with reflections on the scene I had just witnessed; indulging in the recollections which it forced of the simple worship I had been from infancy accustomed to; and wondering at the proneness of military nations and proud sects, to convert the temple of their God into a place of arms, and frighten at the point of the bayonet each better thought that should rise in purity to Heaven.

CHAPTER II.

The crowd of associations which hurried across my brain seemed to bring with them the necessity of fresh air and a green-wood walk. I felt the cramped streets too narrow for me; and knowing that go in what direction I might, I should soon reach the limits of the town, and come to the elm-planted promenade of the ramparts, I moved forward, and quickly gained an opening that led me fairly upon them. The day had brightened up, but the earth was still wet, and I had the consolation of seeing the whole extent of the rampart deserted, except by two or three sentinels, moving their human machinery of arms and legs in the nooks of the bastions, where they had to pace out their hours of watch. I stopped for an instant at the head of a flight of wooden steps, inserted into the inner face of the mound, and I cast down alternate looks upon the crowded town which it defended and the dreary country which it shut out. An embrasure, from which a cannon of large calibre projected, permitted me a view of the ditch and drawbridge, as well as a partial peep at the face of the covered way. In the ditch below, which was quite dry, and converted into an extensive kitchen garden, an inhabitant of the suburb was dressing up a plot of vegetables. A few peasants in starched caps, slouched hats, blue coats or bodices, breeches or petticoats, as the case might be, were clattering with their heavy *sabots* across the bridge, and disappearing under the massive portal. The brick walls at each side had their level faces pitted here and there by the marks of cannon shot, by which the town had been assailed in the short and decisive campaign of the preceding spring. But these skin-deep traces, and the crumbling remains of a couple of earth-formed redoubts, a few hundred yards in front of the place, were the only actual mementos of war. The sullen looking cannons, their heaps of rusty balls beside them, and the plodding sentries pacing backwards and forwards, were mere mechanical appurtenances of what might be either quiet parade or deadly strife. I defy fate to place a man in a position where martial glory and its instruments could present a meaner or less imposing aspect.

Coming close after the scene I had left behind, few situations could be more favourable to that train of prosing philosophy which will force itself, when least called for, upon the observer who has nothing to do but think. I felt, accordingly, falling fast into a mingled labyrinth of metaphysics and morality, when my attention was caught by a figure approaching me from the most distant visible part of the rampart.—I soon discovered it to be that of an old *religieux*; and, as I distinguished the flowing drapery of his black serge dress, his small cocked hat carried in one hand, his prayer book in the other, and the silvery locks which floated out from beneath his black leather scull-cap, I recognized him for the priest, whose interference with the drummers had attracted my attention during the chant of the *Te Deum.* After a time he stopped and looked around him, and, his vision not being quite as sharp as mine, he seemed satisfied that he was alone and unobserved. He therefore folded the drapery of his cassock still closer to his person, put his hat more securely under his arm, opened his missal, threw a glance towards heaven, crossed himself, and began to read. His devotion was instantaneous and intense. So much so that he passed close enough under the branches of the tree against which I leaned, to admit of the rain drops pattering upon the page, without his observing me or appearing sensible to the falling moisture. He took several short turns in this abstracted mood, muttering aloud his pious and rapid invocations; and I at length, from an impulse of curiosity, or something less frivolous perhaps, resolved to break in upon his occupation and accost him. I accordingly, after a forced cough sufficiently loud to excite his observation, took off my hat and addressed him in the respectful tone habitual, I suppose, to every one who approaches age and piety, yet with a manner verging sufficiently on the familiar to shew that I meant something more than a mere passing salutation. He stopped short, looked full upon me an instant, as if striving to recollect my face, closed the book, and replied to my address in terms of simple civility and with a benevolent air. The first step thus taken, I really did not well know how to make a second; and I felt that momentary embarrassment likely enough to follow an actual breach of the ice—the common illustration of such a case. My old companion, however, was one of the last persons in the world with whom a man might be subject to a fit of awkwardness. He had not an atom of the feeling which makes some people take pleasure in seeing others ill at ease with themselves. He was too humble in heart to imagine himself for an instant an object of restraint on any one; and more happily still, he had a fluency of thought and tongue which was of all things the most convenient for allowing those he talked with to recover their self-possession. He therefore completely took the lead in the colloquy; and his loquacity flowed on for some time in a quiet stream of common-place remarks, on the weather and other topics of conversational trade, which every one may deal in without much sense or any licence.

In the very short replies which I here and there edged in, there was no room for a betrayal of my foreign pronunciation; but I had no sooner uttered half-a-dozen sentences together, in the way of commentary on some twenty or thirty which he had poured forth consecutively, than he made corresponding pauses of foot and tongue, and laying his hand gently on my arm, he looked steadily for a moment in my face, and asked me if I were not English. I made an assenting bow, which he replied to by a nod of the head, a "hem," and a half-smothered sigh that sounded hoarsely hollow as it escaped him. He stepped on at a brisker pace than before, occasionally shaking his head, uttering such imperfect sounds as the one just described, and striking his hand at times against his thigh and his breast. It was evident that some painful feeling was labouring within, and from a sharp observation of the workings of his countenance, I saw that but very little excitement was wanting to make him give vent to his emotions in a fit of passion or a flood of tears. Not willing to lead him into such a betrayal of weakness, I endeavoured to resume the thread of our discourse, without weaving a web for his irritability; and I calmly remarked, that I was conscious of the many causes for animosity between his nation and mine.

"My *nation!*" retorted he, with emphasis; and then, after a short pause, his countenance taking a melancholy expression, and his eyes filling up brim-full, he added—"Do me the pleasure, my dear sir, not to use so insulting an epithet in allusion to the miserable colony which my country now is of yours."

I did not know which to be most surprised at in this speech,—the strong feeling of political sensibility, so uncommon in the priesthood, or the deep acknowledgment of national degradation, so unusual in Frenchmen of any class. Determined to bind up the self-inflicted wounds of my companion's pride, I began a train of such soothing observations, as were likely, I thought, to effect that object. I ventured some remarks upon the native richness of the country in soil and productions—the bravery of its men—its historical recollections—and I should have gone much further had not the priest abruptly stopped me with—"For the love of God, Sir, cease! I do not think you mean to hurt my feelings, but this is a weak point with me. I am old and hot-tempered, and can little bear to think of the fertile fields of my country trampled down by English soldiers, nor of her brave youths fighting for English pay against her, nor of her historical recollections, darkened over by divisions and disgrace—this is a theme I cannot talk or think on calmly."

He spoke this with a vehemence that seemed quite to carry him away. His grey eyes flashed fire, and his white hair shook wildly with the rapid motion of his head. His words came out thick and obstructed, and his accent, which was in the former part of our conference particularly pure, and even elegant, was changed by his emotion into something boisterous and coarse. I gazed on him with wonder, for even his physiognomy struck me as no longer the same. There was a turbulent vigour of expression more strong than the fire of French vivacity; and his quivering lip and strained muscles spoke a language less refined than the civilized contortions of French features. Altogether, his person, his gestures, and above all, the words that escaped him, reminded me more of a country then far away from me, than of that in which I was placed at that time. The whole scene brought full upon my mind the memory of my native land; and the reader must excuse the egotism which openly avows what my scribblings have no doubt long since sufficiently betrayed, but which never struck the old priest as a fact, until I formally confessed it to him. As soon as he seemed recovered enough to comprehend me, I exclaimed, "Ah! my good Father, you know not what a chord you have touched. In pourtraying the temporary degradation of your own country, you have but too truly depicted the long enduring wretchedness of mine. And had I been addressing your words to another, he would not have doubted that I rapidly sketched the outlines of Ireland's woe-worn portrait."

While I began this sentence, his looks flashed wildly again, but as I ended, a fixed stare of surprise, accompanied by a relaxation of feature, took place of his former angry sternness of mien.

"I don't exactly understand you," said he eagerly; but recovering in a degree his former tone and accent, "you told me you were an Englishman—didn't you?" "I certainly did, good father, tacitly acknowledge your conjecture as to my nation; but you know there is no distinction for us here: we are all English on the Continent; but I am, I must confess it—an Irishman."

Scarcely was this last word uttered by me, when—how shall I express my astonishment—the old priest started back—then, throwing aside both hat and prayer book, sprang forward,—opened his arms—flung them round my neck—burst into tears;—and with a broad, rich, genuine Irish brogue, exclaimed in English, that bore no taint of *foreign* accent. "An Irishman—an Irishman! you an Irishman! and I after taking you all the while for English—for an inimy! Oh murther, murther, it's too bad entirely. For the love of Jasus forgive me, my jewel—my heart's chuck full of joy and sorrow An Irishman! Oh the devil a doubt of it—long life to your potaty face, it spakes for you plain enough! an Irishman! Oh murther, murther!"

Great as was his surprise, it could not have equalled mine, although its expression was somewhat more extravagant. I found it hard to reconcile my belief to the evidence of the metamorphosis which I witnessed; and I fear I shall have a difficult task, to persuade my readers of the reality of the scene. The change was complete, not only of tone and manner, but it seemed also of character and appearance. The pure French accent and suavity of diction, and the polished air and bearing of a perfect gentleman, were at once converted, as if by magic, into the sweeping overflowings of Hibernian rusticity and warm-heartedness. Both characters seemed equally his in all the shades of their wide distinction; the one not for an instant blending with the other, and each adapted to him in its turn as if no other could by possibility be his. It was quite marvellous to me, and I gazed on him as a kind of phenomenon.

After he had embraced me a dozen times, uttering at every pause incoherent sentences of astonishment and delight, I recovered myself sufficiently to demand some explanation of this double transformation. "Why at least," said I, "did you not address me in English, when I acknowledged myself to be a British subject?"

"What! do you think then," replied he with warmth, "that I would bemean myself so far before an Englishman, as to speak his language and to proclaim myself his slave, when I could talk French and avow myself his inimy!"

"But when you addressed me you evidently spoke of Ireland, and felt only of her!"

"'Troth that's true enough, agrah! but I thought I had the pleasure all the while of cutting the cowld hard heart of a Sassanach, without plainly telling him he was my master; and, after all, France is little better nor Ireland now-a-days. They serve her as they plase, and as she well deserves, to tell the truth of it—but one doesn't like to confess that these English have right on their side any way."

The bitter tone of this speech told as plainly as the words the inveterate hatred of the simple and honest minded speaker, and as our conversation warmed, I came into the gradual knowledge of the peculiarities of his situation, and the singleness of his heart. The wonderful contradiction of his manner, when viewed in the different aspects which I have attempted to show to my readers was easily accounted for, when I learned that he had left Ireland fifty years before, at the age of fifteen, and had ever since that time lived entirely in France; inhaling with the prejudices of the country continual nutriment for those more properly his own, and, while acquiring a perfect knowledge of the language not losing one tone peculiar to his native utterance and accent; his manner of acting as well as speaking had become quite French, while his habits of thought and feeling were still strictly Irish. Some peculiar faculty of memory allowed him to learn a new language, without in the least degree losing the old; and he presented the most extraordinary instance of a double identity that ever came under my observation.

There was one peculiar characteristic about him which was ludicrous in a high degree. While speaking French his words seemed culled with the minutest variety of selection, and not a syllable crept in that bore the slightest relation to impiety or freedom of speech. When he spoke English every sentence was thickly larded with phrases of the lowest rank in the diction of Ireland, and with oaths of the very coarsest kind. The fact was, that he spoke the first language as it had been taught him in a convent, and the latter as he had learned it in bogs and mountains. The one had all the restraint and elegance of art, the other the untutored energy of nature. In Ireland, he had been little better than a peasant; in France, he became a gentleman; and I could dwell, *for* page after page, in *efforts* to describe and account *for* the facility with which he preserved and shifted each distinctive character—like a man slipping *from* his *fustian* shooting-jacket into his silk dressing-gown, and seeming equally at home in each.

I am almost ashamed to confess my regret that I cannot commit his oaths to print; because I feel that my samples of his conversation lose more than half their flavour deprived of those coarse exclamations, which he uttered quite unconsciously, and which, from him, were as harmless as the softest lispings of innocence. I may at least, *salvo pudore*, give some of his less offensive quotations, with his peculiar translations of them,—for he was a poet as well as a priest.

"Oh, my darling!" exclaimed he, with a thundering oath; "never—never forget your country, or abandon her in her distress. High or low, rich or poor, on fut or a-horseback, remember the parent that bore you.—

'*Antiquam exquirite matrem.*'
'Seek out your ould mother,
You'll find no such another.'

That's *Ireland*,—ould Ireland, my darling, as she is called now-a-days; or, Inisfail, Inisalga, Jerna, Juverna, Iris or Erin, as our forefathers, the Milesians, used to call her in other and better days than ours. You'll never forget her, will you?" continued he, with great earnestness.

"I hope I never shall, my good father," replied I, scarcely able to repress a smile which seemed to rise to my lips, from a mixed feeling in which pleasure was predominant.

"*Hope* you won't! be sure of it, my jewel, if you'd expect good luck in this unfortunate world. No good can come of the man that ever forgets his country, abroad or at home. Remember what Horace tould us,

'*Cœlum non animum mutant qui trans mare currunt.*'

'They change their skies, but not their hearts,
Who cross the seas to foreign parts.'"

"Remember that, agrah; and don't be worse nor the Romans. You wouldn't, would you?"

"No, not willingly," said I.

"Not *at all*, you mean," cried he briskly; "don't be saying the thing by halves. Let patriotism be patriotism, out and out. It never does no good when it's split into halves. Remember that we're scattered over the face of the world, true enough,—driven out of our beautiful island,—banished from the greenest spot on earth,—

> '*Nos patriæ fines, et dulcia linquimus arva.*'
>
> 'We quit our beautiful country's bounds,
> Like hunted hares before the hounds.'

But that's no raison why we shouldn't come round to our *forms* again. Saint Patrick forgive me! (and Virgil too!) for a free translation and a joke, at the cost of my country and eclogue the first. But the joke's a bitter one; and what's worse, it's a true one. God help us!"

Such, with the exception of the oaths, which my companion unconsciously vollied forth, and which I listened to with fear lest the ramparts might echo them to some scandal-catching ear, was the general tenor of an hour's discourse. If the patriotism of the honest creature I conversed with ever slumbered, it did so like a hare with its eyes open, and was in an instant ready to spring forth at the slightest excitement. Country was with him indeed a fertile soil, and brought forward, at each mention, a plentiful crop of quotations and translations, the most distorted and ludicrous. He cited, without mercy, Tacitus, Camden, and the venerable Bede, Rhodagonus, Stanihurst, Giraldus Cambrensis, and all other writers, ancient and modern, upon Ireland, to prove what was never, I believe, doubted,—that her soil was the most fertile and least productive, her position the most favourable and least advantageous, and her people the most governable, and worst governed, of any in the world. From these, and other points of a general nature, he branched off into occasional mention of his personal concerns, connections, and adventures; gave ancestral sketches of his family, from the days of Milesius down to those of his own father and name-sake, Mister Dennis O'Collogan, of Sheelanabawn; and made himself acquainted with as much as I knew of *my* family, which was just enough to convince him that its comparatively mushroom growth, its English origin, and above all, its religion, were barely sufficient to give me the title of an Irishman by courtesy, but no more *claim* to it than a man whose birth, parentage, and education had been confined to an island in the Indian Archipelago.

Two circumstances connected with this subject gained me, however, a degree of favour in his eyes, which common causes could never have produced. The first was, when in answer to his enquiry,—"If I had ever heard tell of such a place as the Bog of Allen?" I replied, that I had been born, or at least nursed, upon its borders;—that the whistling of the wind across its brown bleak breast, and the shrill cries of the curlews that sprung from its heather into the skies, were the first sounds that impressed themselves upon my recollection;—that the blackened ruins of Castle Carbery, rising far upon its skirts, were the earliest objects on which my memory seemed to have reposed;—and that its fragrant wild-flowers and mossy banks had been many a time my pillows in the dreamless sleep of infancy. The next matter which endeared me to the friendship of father O'Collogan, was the mention of my *name*. He was too well informed on the affairs of Ireland not to feel that *it* had been naturalized there, by nearly half a century of connection with all that concerned the country's good; and he did honour, for its sake, to one who bears it with a pride that is deeply blended with humility.

The result altogether of our conference was an invitation from father O'Collogan to dine with him in his private lodging; and I felt myself both inclined and entitled to accept of his hospitality.

CHAPTER III.

"THIS is the house," said my inviter, as he stopped before a wretched looking habitation, in a narrow lane close behind the church.

"Do you live *here*, my good Sir?" asked I.

"Where else would I live but in my own lodging?" *answered* he, in the Irish fashion; and, tucking up his cassock high above his knees, he stepped over the thick puddle which lay stagnant before the entrance, mounted the half dozen broken steps leading up to it, and then sidled his broad shoulders through the little passage which led into the dark recesses of the place. I observed him to cross himself as he went in; and, looking up, saw in a niche over the porch, in which there was no door, a little image in plaister of Paris, representing a female with a child in her arms, daubed all over with red and green paint, decked in some tarnished fringe and faded silk for drapery, and a bunch of twisted leaves around the head, withered and wasted into a mockery of what once was flowers. On a stone tablet beneath was carved in the rudest possible chiselling,

Si l'amour de Marie est dans ton cœur gravê
Bon chrétien arrête, et lui dire un Avé.

I afterwards learned that this caricature of the virgin and her babe was placed as a protection from the attacks of robbers, and was supposed of sufficient efficacy to supply the place of a door; and I have since frequently observed that these effigies are almost invariably to be seen placed on dwellings where no temptation to robbery could exist, or where a rational defence was beyond the purchase of the inhabitants.

I worked my way along the ragged floor of

the passage, following closely on the heels of my conductor, whose tall figure and outstretched arms were just visible as he groped along.

"'Take care of the steps, my jewel," cried he, as I stumbled up the first of a flight of stone stairs which he was rapidly ascending.

"I'll take care of myself if I can," replied I, laying hold of the rickety banisters with one hand, feeling my way against the wall with the other, and following as quickly as possible the strides which he was making upwards. The moonbeams glimmering through the remnant of a sheet of brown paper on an unmended window-frame near the first landing place, enabled me to proceed more securely on the ascent; which long habit had rendered so familiar to the priest's tread, as to make light quite unnecessary to him. He seemed to have no notion of my knowledge of the place being more limited than his own; and he neither made apology for the miserable appearance, nor used ceremony in our accompaniment of it

On the third, which was indeed the attic story, he paused, and taking from his pocket a key of most unwieldy dimensions, and the rudest specimen of French manufacturing clumsiness, he opened a door and invited me to walk into his *apartment* as he called it. I entered, and took my place on one of three crazy rush-bottomed chairs, which, with a ricketty little table and a small old-fashioned carved *secretaire*, formed the visible furniture of the room. A faded green striped curtain hanging before a recess, concealed, as I afterwards found out, a *lit de sangle*, that is a bedstead of the meanest construction, which, covered with bedding perfectly corresponding, composed the couch where the worthy tenant of the garret passed nights of pure tranquillity that monarchs might have envied. A couple of coarse prints of our Saviour and the Virgin were fastened with wafers against the white-washed wall; a box-wood crucifix stood upon the mantel-piece; three or four torn books lay on a shelf in the corner; and a *reparation* for fire-lighting filled the hearth, in the shape of two small pieces of wood with some shavings, supported behind by an apparently substantial log, which my accustomed eye soon however detected for one of those stone imitations of faggots known by the name of *Buches Economiques.* The only window of the room was placed in a position the most disadvantageous to the common purpose of a window, for it was directly facing the high wall of the old church, and instead of admitting the rays of the sun and a view of the heavens, it only displayed the discoloured stones of the tottering edifice, and a couple of those hideous faces, neither of men nor beasts, which topple grinningly over the parapets of gothic structures.

"Well, my darling," cried father O'Collogan, rubbing his hands and looking hospitality personified, "you see I'm snug enough here, and heartily welcome you are to the share of it. It isn't much that a man wants in this dirty world, and in troth, I've nothing to complain of: I'm comfortable and contint. Would you like me to light the fire? Not that the day's cowld at all, at all—but may be you'd like a bit of a blaze?"

Before I could answer this question, put in so very questionable a way, a gust of wind forced in the leaves of old books which were substituted for more than one square of broken glass in the window; and these paper panes fluttering and flapping against the frame, answered more plainly than I could.

"Well then, bad luck to that thievish *spalpeen* of a glazier, that won't come and put putty on this paper to keep it in its place! One would think it was a windy day, but it's nothing at all more nor a little breeze that's just turning the corner of the steeple—but may be you're cowld? Would you like a fire, agrah?" said the priest.

"Why, faith, Sir," answered I, "I think a cheerful blaze in the chimney would not be amiss."

"And why didn't you say so?" cried he

briskly, opening at the same time a drawer in the little table, and taking out a tinder-box. "There's nothing aisier, nothing in the world," continued he, hammering a flint against a broken segment of an old horse shoe. His tinder at length caught the spark, and he immediately lighted a match and applied it to the shavings, which as quickly sent out a volume of thick smoke that was met half way up the chimney by "the little breeze," which rolled it back in suffocating volleys into the room.

"Why then the devil fetch that dirty little blackguard of a sweep," exclaimed my host, "that nothing can get him to clain that chimney! but it's well the glazier didn't mend the window after all, for if he did, we must have been obliged to open it. It'll all pass out of the broken panes immediately, my dear, don't be unaisy. I know the ways of the place. Would you just excuse me for five minutes, while I go into the closet to take off my things, and all will be right by and bye?"

I bowed consent, and he opened a door that admitted him into a little place, which seemed about the depth of a common sized cupboard; and while changing his dress, he left me to ruminate in the smoke, on the comparative demerits of glaziers and chimney-sweepers, currents of air, and ill constructed funnels. My reflections would probably have taken a turn somewhat more solid and tangible, had not their progress towards condensation been interrupted by the re-appearance of my host, who very quickly emerged from his retreat. His alteration of costume rather startled me at the first glance, for he seemed once more to have changed with it his character. But a minute or two convinced me that I now saw him in his primitive original aspect, stripped of the fifty years' disguise, that stood with regard to him in that secondary and artificial position, which according to the proverb use does to nature. He had carefully hung his hat and cassock on a peg in his dressing closet, his black leather cap upon another, his high brass-buckled shoes also were deposited on their respective hooks in the partition wall, as well as the cravat and band which had completed his professional attire. He now appeared in a short skirtless jacket of coarse brown woollen, with pantaloons of the same, serving also for stockings, and covering his feet, which were moreover garnished with a worn-out pair of stained cloth slippers, the original colour of which it was beyond my skill to distinguish. His white locks flowed unconfined upon his shoulders, and his open shirt collar shewed a throat still stout and muscular, and the broad bony chest covered thickly with curled grey hair. There was a flush on his gaunt and furrowed cheeks, which seemed to emanate from the same feeling that sparkled in his eyes, and though the feeling might seem to a stranger one of reckless tumult or wild outrage, I saw that it was clearly a blended love of country, and delight in hospitality; the genuine union of national and domestic warmth, so rarely to be found and so hard to be appreciated. His figure and mien taken altogether were as far removed as possible from any theological associations, and he only wanted a shilelah brandished in his hand, to give a perfect notion of an Irish patriarch, leading on his clans to a banquet or a battle, indifferent as to which.

The smoke, after having performed sundry vapoury evolutions under the opposing influences of the chimney and the window, was now quietly taking its regular road to evaporation; and while the priest saw it clearing off, he rubbed his hands together and smiled joyously, taking a chair beside mine and telling me ten times over that I was "heartily, heartily welcome." In a minute or two he started up, as if just recovering the trace of some fugitive thought, opened the room door, and called, in all the civility and mildness of the French language and accent, upon Madame Genevieve, his next neighbour on the same landing place, requesting her "to have the complaisance to occupy herself about preparing his dinner, of which a friend was going to partake, if it did not put her to any inconvenience." Madame Genevieve replied that "she was always ready for the service of *le bon Père Denis*, and that the soup should be on the table in ten minutes." This announcement from her shrill voice was followed by the appearance of her shrivelled face and form, as she tottered in, bent almost double by age, infirmity, and the weight of a coarse brown table-cloth and a couple of napkins. The table was soon arranged by the old priest and this faithful friend and serving woman, who had prepared his frugal meals and attended to his desolate chamber for more than twenty years. Her next entry into the room was with a large earthen pot, called in France a *marmite*, which she deposited by the fire, while she went out again to complete the omelet, for the making of which the said *marmite* was removed from her fire to ours. I knew this was *jour maigre* for the worthy priest, and, as a tureen of onion soup was quickly smoking on the table, I was rather puzzled to divine what were the contents of the pot, until their boiling furiously up against the lid forced it to one side, and I discovered amidst the foam of the agitated water a quantity of large potatoes, dancing in the bubbling element and bursting their skins as if they laughed in concert with the motion.

"My good Father," cried I, not a little pleased at this plentiful specimen of our national food, "I see you have not lost your Irish taste."

"God forbid that I did!" replied he; "no, no, my dear child, there's no fear of my losing the taste of any thing Irish, for I've the smack of the potatoes, and the flavour of the turf just as fresh upon my palate this minute as the day I sailed from the Cove of Cork. Sit over—sit over to the table, my Jewel—Madame Genevieve will be after draining the potatoes while we're aiting our soup."

These operations were duly performed, and when our part was finished the old woman placed her pyramid of *pommes de terre au naturel* in the centre of the table.

"Ah, there they are the smilers, smoking and mailey!" exclaimed the priest. "There they are, just quite as natural as if they came out of my poor ould father's cabbage garden at the fut of Castle Carbery. Why then doesn't this put you in mind of Ireland? upon my salvation it warms the heart in my body, that's no lie that I tell you. Och! that's the real way to dress potatoes—there's none of your *frites* or *purées*, or *maîtres d' hôtel*, but plain honest downright thumpers, bursting out through their skins, and crying 'come ait me, come ait me,' like the little pigs with knives and forks in them."

But I cannot afford more room to a detail of our repast, nor of my host's discourse. The homeliness of both possessed a considerable relish for me; and the natural bearing of the priest while I partook of his humble fare, and listened to his coarse phraseology, put me completely at my ease, because it convinced me that he was perfectly at his.

When we had finished the soup, the omelet, a bit of salt fish, and the "biggest half of the potatoes," as my host expressed it, he stood up and produced from the bottom of a little press in the wall, a bottle covered with dust, and about half full of a colourless liquid. While he proceeded to break off the sealing wax which thickly covered the cork, I saw the tears rush into his eyes, as his countenance became evidently agitated.

"Well then," cried he, "it's a thought that suddenly struck me, and sure it isn't a bad one;—yes, yes, by my sowl, you shall drink share of it, you shall, and you're the first man that has as much as smelt it, for two-and-twenty years. There—smell it, what is it do you think? do you know what it is now—Eh?"

I smelt it and tasted accordingly, and found

that this treasure was nothing more nor less than some exquisite old whiskey, possessing the fine flavour of the peat smoke with which all the illicit spirits made in Ireland is impregnated.

"Ha!" exclaimed I, "this is indeed a treat. How did you come by this, my good father?"

"Never you mind how I came by it, but make yourself a tumbler—Madame Genevieve will give us hot water and sugar immediately.—How I come by it is a long story—but we'll drink to the memory of him who gave it to me, any how; God rest his innocent sowl!"

There was a tone of deep grief in the utterance of this phrase, and I saw the big tears rolling rapidly down the old man's cheeks.

"Aye, aye, rowl away, rowl away," cried he bitterly apostrophising the falling drops, and dashing them off with his hand—"it's right that my ould heart should weep drops of blood if possible, instead of salt water—but even that's not wanting to keep my sorrow fresh—rowl away, rowl away!"

My curiosity being powerfully excited by these words, I ventured to ask who had been the lamented friend whose memory caused him such grief.

"Why, my jewel, he was nothing but a *garde-du-corps*, what you'd call in English, one of the body guard of unfortunate Louis the Sixteenth.—But he was my friend, and a real gentleman bred and born—of as ancient a family, as pure blood, and as brave a heart as any king in Christendom—that's what he was; and the devil such another he left behind him. Here's long life to him—that is, I main, here's long life to his memory, which will never die while there's life in this ould body, any how."

"I pledge your melancholy toast, my dear Sir," said I, "without knowing even the name of your lamented friend."

"His name was Cornelius,"—said the priest solemnly, "that is his Christian name: as to the other, it is not convanient nor necessary to expose an ould and honourable family, though he took good care, poor crathur, that his body should be as free after death as his mind was while he lived—the Lord have mercy upon his unfortunate sowl!"

It would be impossible to convey any notion to my readers of the deep-sounding sensibility which breathed in these expressions, or of the proof which the speaker's manner afforded how natural feeling can overwhelm every impression of the ludicrous or vulgar. A high priest in his pontificals could not have pronounced an invocation in a strain of eloquence more effective than the simple exclamation of my unsearched host. The faint light of a solitary lamp, and the moaning of the wind through the turrets and angles of the church outside, were in keeping with the train of feelings excited by the looks and words of the priest, and they were altogether more solemn than might appear natural to their abrupt development, or even the subject they were linked with.

A few minutes were passed in deep silence,

during which the lips of my companion betrayed by their motion the prayers which he half felt and half uttered. I was intently observing the workings of his countenance, when the deep tone of the church bell roused him up. He started from his seat, exclaiming, "The vesper bell! I must leave you, my dear child, for awhile by yourself—I am rather past my time as it is—but I'll not be long, and you must amuse yourself with this bottle of whiskey and your own thoughts. When I come back I'll tell you more about poor Cornelius—but, stop, may be you'd like to *read* something about him in the main time, would you?"

"You have deeply interested me for your friend," replied I; "and I shall hear or read any thing about him with no common anxiety."

"Well then, open that *secretaire*," said he, "you'll find several bundles of letters and papers in both prose and verse, written partly of him, and to him, and by him. You may turn them all over and over: yours is the first eyes that has looked upon them, barring my own, since the poor fellow tied them up himself in the bundle there. I'm afraid they're rather mouldy and moth-eaten, but you'll see for yourself. God bless and preserve you my honey, till I come back to you, any how."

No sooner had the priest quitted the room, than I took possession of the large pacquet of manuscripts from the secretaire, brought it over to the table, placed a fresh log upon the fire, trimmed the little lamp, and was beginning to read, when the door opened and he suddenly re-appeared. "That's right, my jewel," cried he, "make yourself snug and cozy, and read away till I come back to you—but I'm just stepped in again to tell you that Madame Genevieve will make up a bed for you on the chairs to-night—a shake down as we say in Ireland—you can't think of laving the house, for it's raining cats and dogs outside in the street, so make yourself snug and cozy, mind what I tell you—and mix another tumbler."

"My dear Sir," exclaimed I, "I cannot consent to give you and your old woman all this trouble—really—"

"Hould your tongue, hould your tongue, I tell you. Your trouble's my pleasure, and Madame Genevieve's too, so no more's to be said about it—good evening to you."

With these words he disappeared once more, and I betook myself again to my new studies, not at all sorry at the prospect of passing my night in company with the MSS. however bad my accommodation.

It is scarcely necessary to say how long or how short a time I sojourned in the neighbourhood of Father O'Collogan. My readers would most probably rather hear the story of his friend the *garde-du-corps*. This I shall as usual tell in my own fashion, making use of the scattered papers confided to me for that purpose by the priest, according to my own discretion, and I trust *discreetly*. They consisted of many letters, originals and copies, many leaves of a regular journal, fugitive notions apparently just arrested on their flight, and three or four pamphlets relating to events of more than twenty years before, all put together without the least order, and requiring much trouble and management before they acquired the regular air of the story I am about to present to my readers; and, it may be needless to state that many a hiatus was filled up by the minute details furnished to me by my worthy assistant.

CHAPTER IV.

The principal hero of my story, for its title tells that it has two, was called Cornelius at his baptism, in compliment to a long train of recollections linked to a name which had been borne with pride by many of his ancestors. His family appellation I am not at liberty to record. Its concealment was the only restriction put by Father O'Collogan upon my free-will, in the application of the materials with which he furnished me. It is sufficient to state that it was one of the oldest and most respectable in Ireland, belonging to a family which had been ever famed for its nationality, which had never bought freedom from proscription at the price of dishonour, and which felt its pride regularly increase in proportion as its wealth diminished. Our hero's father was bred in the religion of his ancestors; and although he had long broken from the trammels of the Roman Catholic faith, he felt it a point of honour to maintain an outward adherence to a belief, which persecution had re-adorned in all the attractions that reason had torn from it. Had he renounced it publicly he might have gained wealth and distinction in almost any line of life, for he was a man of an enlightened and powerful mind; but he scorned the wages of an apostacy that might bear the construction of self-interest. He was therefore one among the millions of Irish secured to the church of Rome, by the very means, ill-planned as they were odious, adopted for promoting its subversion. Finding that in his own country he had no chance of advancement, he resolved to enter into the service of some foreign power, and carve out for himself a road to the fame for which he panted. He made choice of France; and he fought under the banners of the lily for ten years. His military career was at this time stopped by severe and almost incurable wounds. He was forced to renounce the hopes of his youth long before they had attained completion; and, while yet within the earlier half of man's measured span, he retired to his native country with the rank of Major, and a reduced but still sufficient income. He there married, but soon lost his wife by death—but was consoled for twenty years by watching the growth, and training the mind of his only son, Cornelius, the hero of our tale. The education of this boy became almost his only occupation. Bad health and broken prospects had brought on an indolence of habit which was not natural to him. He became sedentary and lived secluded. His ancient family mansion, standing on a rock and frowning blackly down upon the fierce Atlantic, whose keen blasts were yearly wearing it away, was rarely visited by the scanty neighbourhood around. The owner repulsed the advances of society, and the place had few attractions, but for him and his young charge. They pursued together a course of study, and amusement of a peculiar kind; irregular and isolated, but effective. On somewhat more than the rudiments of classical learning, Cornelius had engrafted a knowledge of more than one foreign language. He was perfect master of French, which he talked habitually with his father, who not disheartened by his own ill-luck, meant his son to try the same career in which he had broken down. Military topics were therefore the chief theme of their discourse, but others had their share of attention. Field sports held a prominent place in the pursuits of Cornelius; and often, in calm and storm, he boldly committed himself to the ocean, in his little fishing skiff, accompanied by his foster-brother and favourite companion, a wild but faithful youth called Bryan Mulcahie. Cornelius had a natural taste for the arts, which was not left uncultivated by his careful parent. He learned the first principles of design and colouring. He loved music—and often have the tones of his youthful voice, mingling with his father's sonorous notes, held harmony together, on the rocky battlement that raised the singers high above the waves which rushed in hoarse murmurings through the cavities below.

Frequently in their evening loiterings, after they had sung together some mournful ditty, on Irish subjects and in their native language, the father would pause, and repressing a rising sigh or tear, he would make Cornelius look round towards the east, and gaze with him on the wide tract of hill and dale, that was once the possession of their ancestors. Then as their eyes, little by little, sank down on the narrowed spot of ground which fines and confiscation had left to them, the fierce soldier would feel all his energy rise up. He would then in language of deep eloquence, teach his son a lesson of hatred against England; and next by an abrupt transition instil some feeling favourable to France

—the refuge of their race. The intellect of the boy thus nurtured, made daily progress in wild, yet vigorous growth. His father's words sank deep into his heart. In proportion as he shrunk from England and its associations, he naturally turned towards France; and all the day dreams of his youth seemed to rise from the pleasant vineyards, the bright gardens and gay promenades of the country which he looked to as the field of his future hopes. From unhappy Ireland he was taught to expect nothing, for, his family and his kind saw nought in relation to her but disgrace in the past, and despair for what was to come.

Once only during his boyhood, when he was scarcely of an age to comprehend the events that were then acting, one broken beam of gladness seemed to play on the surface of the wretchedness which had so long flooded his country. This was the epoch of 1782, when the rushing eloquence of one great man shook corruption on its very throne, and roused from their inmost recesses every element of that public feeling which seemed to sleep the sleep of death. It was at this period when Cornelius saw his father, in common with all who possessed a spark of patriotism in their hearts, bind on his sword once more, and mingle in the ranks of Ireland's volunteers, that the ardent boy thought his country might yet demand a place among the nations. The faint gleam died away, and a lengthened shadow lay unlit upon the land. Older and wiser heads drooped down once more; but our hero, growing every year into the maturity of enthusiasm, which becomes old ere reason ripens, held proud language and high hopes, while others doubted and despaired. It was about this time that he gave himself up to the indulgence of an uncultured love for poetry, and under the impulse of some strong feelings of resentment for the unmitigated reproaches poured out against his country, he gave vent to his thoughts in the following

STANZAS TO IRELAND.

1.

Aye, let all earth cry out on thee,—all those
Who mark thy red crimes blazoned to the world,
Like the stained Corsair's, whose broad banner glows
Far o'er the outraged seas in blood unfurled.
They hear the blasphemous utterance of thy tongue;
Thy miscreant yells come through the shuddering air:
But all unseen the goad and knotted thong,
Which lash thee on, and drive thee to despair.

2.

As Spartan slaves, wine-maddened by their lords,
Reviled--then scourged into sobriety;
So driven, so drunk with guilt, thy frantic hordes;
So scorn and scourge, my country, fall on thee!
What would thy rulers have from thee? Repose?
Are flowers the crop which ravaged deserts yield?
Or would they reap, from regions steeped in woes,
The harvest springing from Joy's cultured field?

3.

Like some bright blade—the day of battle past—
Flung by, in desolate damps, to rot and rust,
So they who used thy energies have cast
Thee off despised, to let foul crimes encrust
Thy beauteous face; and thence, corroding, eat
Deep to the inmost kernel of thy heart;
And when thy forced deformities they meet,
Cry out, "How rotten and how vile thou art!"

4.

But, as a lorn barge, loosed upon the wave
From the proud ship which bore it on her deck,
Thou yet may'st ride the storm—the billows brave,
Which whirl the fragments of *her* shattered wreck
Down ocean's gulphs; the while thy snow-white sails,
Emblems of purity and peace, are seen
In brighter suns, and fanned by milder gales,
To shine and flutter o'er the Atlantic green.

5.

Thy teeming vales, thy mountain heights sublime,
Where Nature's gifts have all advanced and thriven,
Tell that thou wert not singled out for crime,
Nor branded as earth's shame by angry Heaven.

And must the mighty river of the mind
  Roll refluent back, despite of Nature's plan?
Must all else flourish, nurtured by mankind,
  Save one degenerate growth, and that one—Man?

6.

No—suffering land! Heaven's righteous arm will foil
  The impious author of thy deeds of night;
And o'er the stains of thine ensanguined soil,
  Proud stems of virtue cast their shadows bright!
And shouts may echo yet from thy wild hills,
  Their sides reverberant answering to the plains,
Such tone as that which through the bosom thrills,
  When freedom's trumpet sounds o'er broken chains!

I have selected these lines from many such effusions, to the full as desultory, and still more rebellious; because I think them as much adapted to the state of Ireland in our own time, as they were in that when they were written. But it would appear that the bright anticipations here indulged in, suddenly sunk into that state of hopelessness which I have ascribed as common to the connections of Cornelius. At twenty years of age his tone was totally altered; his verses breathed no more a spirit of ardent expectation, and he embraced with unspeakable delight the offer made to his father, in his behalf, of a commission as garde-du-corps in the service of the king of France. He had been for some time looking out for this appointment. It had been obtained through the interest of his father's military friends at the court of Versailles; and during the interval between the formal demand and its final success, our hero's mind turned, as was natural to his time of life, but more particularly to his individual character, solely and with impassioned ardour on the object directly in its view.

Cornelius was, in the purest meaning of the word, an enthusiast; a youth of genuine, not factitious sentiment,—of high-wrought feelings untinged by prejudice, and free from the spurious vigour which marks the tone of the fanatic. His intellect was expansive, and consequently liberal.

His views were not narrowed, but his affections were. He could take a wide range into the fields of speculative enquiry; but when a passion touched his heart, it instantly absorbed it. He fixed on an object of devotion, and every faculty of his soul seemed centred there, as though one powerful point of attraction had gathered round it each varying tone of sentiment and thought. For this ruling object, be it what it might, he would risk any thing, without calculating what he risked, and sacrifice all, unconscious that he made a sacrifice. In gazing upon it, distance, or time, or obstacles existed not for him. He bounded over space, and spurned impediments. The abstraction of his looks spoke the fulness, not the vacuum of his mind. The fervour of his words sprung from energy, not violence. His individual existence seemed unreal. He neither lived nor moved as of or for himself; for the very plans and purposes of his being seemed dependant on that other impulse, whose movements seemed to lead, although they were not linked with his. Such are the striking characteristics of feeling—the wild forgetfulness of self—the absolute devotedness to somewhat else—be it a person, a passion, a sentiment, or a sensation—which constitute, according to my creed, the frame of thought that may be honored with the term enthusiasm.

But the dignity of such a state of mind is highly dangerous. The state itself is neither sane nor solid. It offers no security for real advantage to the possessor, or rational benefit to others. All its attributes are vapoury, however pure; and while the mortality it is joined with, needs incitements essentially real, it yields but abstractions and vain sounds. To make enthusiasm useful to mankind, it requires a union with those positive feelings of our nature which modify its excess and bring it to the level of human sentiment, while it lifts them above the mark of human weakness. It is thus that enthusiasts are always bad statesmen, and worse patriots. They pursue a phantom, and let slip the substance. They misconceive their object, and miscalculate their means; and in their ideal views of moral cause, they wholly overlook the more material point of physical result. Had the mind of Cornelius been finally devoted to his country's service, the chances are that he would have done her harm instead of good; and that his aspirations after liberty, his philanthropy, his courage and his virtue, might have all, as in an instance later than his time, have led a noble youth into inevitable ruin, forced out his dying breath amidst the horrors of a scaffold, and buried the fresh springing hopes of his country in the imputed ignominy of a traitor's grave.

The destiny of our hero turned him from a fate like this, and a prospect of military fame seemed spreading out before him. Had he followed it to the end there is no knowing what he might have become. A conqueror and a king perhaps!—as it was, he was reserved for something not so elevated certainly, and therefore more within the reach of our sympathy. He, however, unable to foresee his fortunes, plunged boldly into the futurity which his ardent imagination conjured up, and he thought he saw passing before him shadows of glory and greatness, which he afterwards found to have been reflected from no substance. His father was, in a more sober way, almost equally happy. He not only rejoiced for Cornelius's sake in the fair prospect of honorable distinction which was opened to his talents and his courage, but he also felt that deep delight with which a parent gazes on a child of promise, in the irresistible conviction that it is doomed to add to the honor of its race, and to complete those steps towards reputation which he himself may have had the happiness to make. This is one of the purest feelings which can animate a father's breast. It is separate from every tinge of jealously or envy, for we form and fashion out our rival offspring in the hope of his surpassing us, and feel honoured in the anticipation of his superiority. How well it is for fathers that they may not raise the curtain of the future, and weep over the weakness or worthlessness of those who follow them! This last reflection must not however be taken as applying to Cornelius.

The preparations for his departure were soon made. His wardrobe was choice but scanty. His books few but good. His drawing materials, his flute, his gun, a case of pistols, and a few other objects of utility rather than shew completed his equipment. He carried a small sum of ready cash, a letter of credit on a Paris Banker, and three or four of introduction and recommendation to his father's military friends. Among the latter was included one to "Le Père Denis O'Collogan," the former chaplain of that regiment of the Irish Brigade in which Cornelius's father had served, but now removed from military associations, and filling the humble station of curate-assistant to one of the parishes of the town of Versailles, at that epoch the seat of

Government and Royalty, and consequently the destination of our hero.

Cornelius left his home, the narrow circle of his affections and attachments, with feelings of almost unmixed pleasure. His very regrets were rather of a soothing than of a bitter nature; and the tears which gushed from his eyes seemed to flow from a source that did not spring in woe. He looked on his separation from all that he loved, as a joining link to their future meeting, rather than as a breaking off from a connection that was never to be renewed. He glanced quickly over the absence that was to check their intercourse, and pictured the joys of its revival, as the traveller who stands on the edge of some chasm that separates one mountain from another, looks across it at the sunny banks beyond, without reflecting that they may be overcast, while he tracks the weary paths of the ravine, which he must descend and mount before he can reach them. The few servants—the numerous followers—the old nurse—the Parish Priest—all who were connected with the family by internal or external ties, poured blessings on Cornelius as they bade him adieu; and the general hope among the sorrowing group was, that "the Young Master" was one day to return, a great General at the head of a French army to give freedom to his country. His father accompanied him to the sea-port a few miles distant, where he was to take shipping for Nantes. Their only attendant was Bryan Mulcahie. He was to lead back Cornelius's horse, after taking leave of his former companion and play-fellow, of late years transformed more absolutely into his master. Bryan's devotion to Cornelius had been growing more and more every year, but his respect for him had for a long time increased in proportion. Cornelius was greatly attached to him: he thought he possessed one of the most feeling hearts possible, and the bitterest sensation he had on leaving home, was a fear of the effects which his departure would produce on this faithful creature. He saw, as he thought, that poor Bryan was making a fierce struggle with his emotions, for not a symptom of regret had been yet visible, if it was not when just as Cornelius tore himself from the embraces of his weeping nurse the mother of Bryan, the latter could not restrain his tears, but flung himself for an instant into the open arms where Cornelius' retreat had left a void. But soon recovering himself, he was busy in strapping and bridling portmanteaus and horses; and as the party trotted slowly along towards the place of embarkation, he was the only one whose features shewed no trace of care.

The parting between Cornelius and his father was such as befitted a first separation. It would have worn a different aspect had they been aware of what their next meeting would be. Cornelius stepped on board, his father mounted his horse at the sea-side, and thus they parted. But while our hero stood on the deck, and marked his parent ride away, followed by Bryan, the deep sighs which were heaving up his breast, like the billows that lifted the ship upon their bosom, were counterbalanced and checked by a feeling of disappointment and almost of indignation, as he reflected on the indifferent air with which this long cherished foster-brother had borne their separation. Cornelius had been looking for the outbursting of his uncultured emotions, and as he saw him bustling about, busying himself in the ship, and talking to the sailors, he was sure that the sequel to these artificial constraints would have been a scene of painful excess. But Bryan did not shed a tear. When his young master, scarcely able to suppress his own, stretched out his hand to him, he shook it cordially, and as Cornelius with a broken voice bade him farewell, and hoped that they might meet again, his answer was simply, "Troth and I hope we will, Sir—Long life to you, Master Cornalius!" and he threw him a nod as he put his foot on the stirrup, which said nothing more nor less than the most common place "Good bye!"

The sun was down, and the sharp air of an evening late in April curled the surface of the sea, and forced the mimic breakers against the pier close to which the vessel lay. Cornelius as he lost sight of his father had no inducement to remain on deek. He went down to his berth, and his last reflection as he stepped below was given to the uncertainty of friendship and affection. "Good God," cried he, "if this unsophisticated youth—this untaught companion of my earliest hours—bound to me by so many ties of gratitude and love—can part from me thus unconcerned, what am I to expect from the heartless connections of society! Can I reckon on any friendship after this? It is a bitter lesson—but a good one, perhaps, on the threshold of the world!"

In an hour the ship had left her moorings, and she swept gallantly on her course with a favouring breeze.

CHAPTER V.

On the evening of the third day the coast of France was in sight, Ushant, and the sand heaps, which seemed rising from out of the shore, and looked red in the reflection of the setting sun. The sailing had been hitherto smooth and pleasant, and Cornelius, being the only passenger, had had the little cabin entirely to himself, and the deck nearly so. He had enjoyed this short and solitary voyage. He had felt, or fancied, his mind to acquire fresh power in the sensation of singleness forced on him by this new position. He liked the idea of being alone in the world; and he felt as if he could track his course through it, impelled by the breath of Fate, as freely as the barge he sailed in cut its way through the waters, under the influence of the breeze that urged it on. He stretched himself in his berth this third night, rather more disappointed than gratified at the announcement of the master, that they should anchor in the Loire the next morning. This calculation was, however, unfulfilled. A sudden squall came on at midnight, followed by a total change of wind and a heavy gale. At day-break, when Cornelius went on deck, the little vessel had changed her course. She was standing out to sea, and a thick haze shut out the view of the shore. He was pleased at this new turn in the tide of events. He liked the prospect of the sea in this novel aspect, so different from the in-shore experience which he had hitherto had of storms. He kept the deck for two days while they laboured through what is called the Chops of the Channel, and almost the only object that took off his attention from the observation of clouds and billows was one of the sailors, the youngest of the scanty crew, whom he remarked to pay repeated and evidently stolen visits to the hold, with, at first, constant supplies of food, and afterwards with every thing to be had likely to bring any alleviation to the sufferings of sickness, such as pork broth, some tea warmed in a greasy saucepan, and other remedies quite as unpalatable. Cornelius, pleased with the lad's humanity, questioned him as to the object of his care, but received for answer in a hesitating tone, that it was nothing but a dog that he had brought over unknown to the Captain, and he entreated our hero's secrecy, which was faithfully promised. As the voyage and the gale continued, Cornelius compassionated the poor animal below, for he frequently heard, as he thought, the low-moaned utterings of its distress. A piteous whine used sometimes to murmur through the water-casks, as if the suffering brute was conscious of its concealment, and now and then when the captain was busied in a distant part of the deck, and that the young sailor could slip towards the prison-house, and whisper a word of kindness below, Cornelius fancied that he heard the dog howl freely at one of the portholes that opened on the starboard side of the ship.

This voyage did not last long enough to make it monotonous. Another day enabled the captain to bear up for Dieppe; and the weather was tolerably calm and dry when the vessel shot past the pier, and under the guidance of a pilot who had come out to meet her, she ran safely up to the quay, and came to quiet anchorage. Before even they had crossed the bar and entered the harbour, a boat had come alongside, and been fastened by a rope to the ship, by the custom-house and police-officers with which it was filled. Four or five of these were soon on deck, demanding from the captain, a rough round little Irishman with a red face, a state of his crew and other papers; knowing these formalities, he had prepared himself the required documents, and handed them a list containing his own name, those of six men, and the before-mentioned lad who composed the crew, as well as that of our hero the sole passenger. This was strictly examined, and the persons mentioned scrutinized one by one. Some questions next followed as to cargo, which the Captain answered by pointing to his bills of lading and certificates; and to some other enquiries he replied, with rather a choleric tone and strong gestures of discontent, "me no savez, me no savez," which rather dubious phrase constituted his whole stock of that mixture of languages approaching the nearest to French. The smiles of the officers irritated him exceedingly, and when Cornelius interpreted their next enquiry, "whether there were any contraband goods on board?" the little Captain's indignation was excessive, and he used sundry violent and abusive terms as they went down to make a thorough search, beginning at the cabin. There they found nothing; but as they prepared to descend into the hold, our hero observed that the countenance of the young sailor shewed considerable confusion and agitation. He thought that it was more than was called for by the discovery of a dog, even if it had been contraband, and he began to fancy that there was something more serious in this mysterious circumstance than had appeared at first. The officers went down—the young sailor stood silent, but with his looks earnestly straining after them—and in a few minutes two of them came upon deck, declaring that "all was right." The lad seemed to breathe more freely; but was in an instant more agitated than ever, when one of those who remained below hallooed out in a loud voice for the captain, as he was sure that there was some person concealed in the hold. "What does he say?" cried the captain to Cornelius. "What does he say?" echoed the young sailor. Cornelius told them. "He lies, d—n him!" cried the captain. "I am ruinated entirely, out and out!" sobbed the boy. Cornelius stepped forward, rather interested in the scrutiny, and feeling an instant conviction that this youth had most probably carried away with him some sweetheart from the Irish coast whom he hoped to smuggle over undiscovered, a very common occurrence with sailors, particularly of that nation. Upon calling to mind the plaintive sounds which he had listened to for the last two days, Cornelius was convinced they had proceeded from a human being. He was only astonished at his dullness in having suffered himself to be deceived. The particular nature of his surprise may then be imagined, when he saw lugged upon deck, between two of the searchers, the almost inanimate and totally exhausted figure of Bryan Mulcahie. Sea-sickness and confinement had given him a most cramped and cadaverous look. His face was pale, and his limbs were quite distorted. But as the fresh air blew upon him he seemed instantaneously revived, and when the officers loosed their hold, he threw himself at the feet of his astonished master, clung to his knees, and blubbered out prayers for forgiveness and protection. Our hero looked on in a mixture of contending feelings, surprise, pleasure, and compassion being uttermost. The officers stormed, blasted, bellowed, thundered; and muttered threats of confiscation, imprisonment, the galleys, and the gallows. The little captain was almost stupified with wonder and rage. The culprit sailor was confessing, and crying, and supplicating. The whole scene was one of extreme confusion, and to our hero, of considerable interest. "Good heaven," cried he to Bryan, "what persuaded you to take this step and endure all this misery?"

"Och, blur an' ouns! Master Cornalius, and is it you that's after axing me that? Did you think then I was going to come for to lave you—to go all alone by yourself into a strange country, with nobody at all at all to look after you? Ah, little it is that you know of me, if you suspected me of such a dirty turn!"

"But to leave your mother in this way, Bryan! Did you tell her of your intention?"

"Why then what the devil do you take me for, Master Cornalius? Tell her anagh! Troth and it's me that didn't. Sorrow's the word I spoke to the poor ould crathur, good or bad, but that kiss that I give her when we were laving the ould Castle—God's luck be wid it, and wid her too—and wid the master—and wid—"

"And my father—you told him, did you?"

"Why then I tould nobody at all, I tell you, Master Cornalius. What's the use of your wanting to make me out a fool? Troth I left the poor master trotting along towards home by himself, and dropped back a little, pretending I was crying after your honour, and that's the way I slipt back and came aboord, never saying nothing to no one but to Jemmy Toole there, the cabin-boy, who promised to give me my passage, lodging, aiting, and drinking, free, gratis, for nothing at all—and the devil a much more it was worth, to spake God's truth of it—so you see, Sir, I'll not cost you a farthing after travelling so far together."

Cornelius was of a different opinion, for he foresaw a great deal of trouble in the affair, the officers becoming every moment more clamorous. He explained to them the whole circumstances of the case, but produced little effect on them, for they were disposed to treat the business almost as seriously as if it had been a matter of high treason. Cornelius saw nothing for it but to submit to all that might happen, and he was on the point of consenting to the captain, the cabin-boy, and Bryan being marched on shore, prisoners of state, when the latter called out to our hero, "why then, blur an' age, Master Cornalius, why don't you shew them your commission? What the devil's the good of your being a captain, if you can't have a sarvent to follow you without his being clapped into jail like a common rogue? Och then, to the devil I pitch such a thieving country, if that's the way wid it."

Conelius took the hint—avowed his situation—and saw in an instant the immense value of the consequence which is given by common consent from all the subalterns of government to those whom they consider as making part of the system. The whole affair was arranged on the spot; Bryan's name added to the muster-roll as the servant of Cornelius: Jemmy Toole absolved of crime, and rewarded into the bargain by our hero; the captain acquitted of connivance; the formalities of disembarkation facilitated; the passports of Cornelius and his domestic made out, and both of them, that very evening, pursuing their route towards Versailles, one of them on the roof, and the other inside of the carriage that conveyed the Government courier, who was to deliver his despatches at the court the following morning.

Cornelius's reflections on taking possession of his place in the carriage were of a nature far different from those with which he had commenced his sea voyage. The devoted attachment of Bryan, his voluntary exile from his native land, his abandonment of his mother, and his cheerful endurance of the miseries he had already suffered, were ample guarantees for his future fidelity. Our hero felt his thoughts to flow, as it were, in a different channel. He blamed the selfish and cynical turn of mind that he had been cherishing for some days past, and he looked forward into life, convinced that the finer feelings of the heart must form the chief delights of its unexplored mysteries Bryan was so tired from the effects of the voyage, and of a most hearty meal to which his recovered appetite did ample justice on landing, that he slept soundly all night; and both master and man were astonished when they found themselves, about eight o'clock the next morning, fairly entering the suburbs of Versailles, and thus at the end of their journey, before they had had time almost to mark its progress, or adjust themselves to its commencement.

The sudden arrival into the heart of a foreign land, amidst a strange people and a new climate, where every thing wears an air of novelty that almost seems unnatural, is to every one a matter of much marvel. But to one of Cornelius's frame of mind it was something more than that. He seemed to himself to have been magically wafted into a new state of being. Bryan was stupified; and gazed and gaped and listened with open eyes and mouth and ears.

The morning of this arrival formed a memorable epoch in the annals of France. It was the 4th of May, 1789, the day previous to the first assembling of the States General. The season bore a strict analogy to the state of the political world, for it was the spring-time of hope to all the thinking part of mankind. The principle of moral liberty had been rapidly spreading across the earth, and under its broad and sheltering wings the States General of France were now assembling, to regenerate society and place men and monarchs in the relative positions which they ought to occupy for each others good. It was a grand experiment; and the pulse of the world beat high, but steadily, in expectation of the result. Necker, the minister who planned the assembly, was lauded and condemned—accused and almost deified—according to the varying passions and wishes of men. The fact is, that Necker acted wisely and well. His mental vision was far-seeing but not omniscient; and he was as one who gazes on the wide expanse of ocean, but may not penetrate the under-currents which wind beneath its surface. The state of things called out for the experiment, and it was about to be tried under the most splendid auspices. The world was all excitement and agitation—a crisis was prepared; every thing promised fair and well. The people knew and claimed their rights. Louis, the representative of European monarchy, neither hoped nor wished to retain his unnatural power. The well being of the world was at issue—wisdom did all that it could calculate—but, as must ever be the case in public projects, the rest was left to chance.

Nothing could exceed the splendor of the preparations made at Versailles on this occasion.

The whole population of Paris and the country for leagues around poured into this town, which was the seat of government and the scene of this unrivalled exhibition. The concourse was prodigious. The houses were decorated with every possible symbol of joy. Festoons of flowers hung gracefully across the streets. Every garden was rifled of its treasures, and the earliest roses of the season were profusely scattered abroad. Arches of triumph and altars were constructed in the open places; and every nook hung out its piece of carpet, its white flag, or its bouquet in humble effort to do honour to the king, and the representatives of a people, willing to be ruled, and worthy of being free.

The official situation of Cornelius, and the courier with whom he travelled, ensured him a passage through the wide and early crowded streets—and he was enabled freely to gaze on the splendid avenues tree-planted at each side, and the noble ranges of houses, of a style of architecture superbly novel to his observation.

They passed with a rapid pace towards the palace, where the offices of the ministers were held; and the admiration of our hero, as they hurried through the throng, was equalled by *its* astonishment at the picture of grotesque and stupified amazement presented by Bryan Mulcahie, as he sat perched with wondering looks on the top of the cabriolet. To prove the near affinity of the ludicrous with the magnificent, Cornelius's reflections on all that surrounded him, were irresistibly mingled with the recollections of his servant's costume, a large grey *frize* coat thrown loosely over a jacket and waistcoat of the same stuff, with corduroy breeches and a pair of rude gaiters, partially shewing his dark blue woollen stockings—the ordinary undress of Bryan while performing his out-door work at *the Castle*, and the only suit with which he thought of providing himself on his abrupt departure. Our hero's first care, therefore, on taking possession of the apartment, to which he was immediately appointed in the barracks of the Garde-du-Corps, after presenting himself to the commandant of his troop, was to send for a tailor to furnish Bryan with a suit of livery; and he left him with strict injunctions not to leave the room until his return. This affair, and the operation of unpacking, dressing, breakfasting, and settling in their new quarters, had occupied some hours, and it was more than noon when Cornelius set out to throw himself amongst the crowd, and gaze, in that solitude, on the mass of splendid wonders around him. He resolved not to attempt any visit at such a time to any of those to whom he had letters; preferring to mingle with the observers of what was going on, and taking chance for being satisfied in the scanty enquiries which he was inclined to make—for the amazement with which he was filled, seemed to raise him above the pettiness of detail.

Following the course of the living tide, he was soon in the great space opposite the front entrance of the palace; and gaining an elevation close to the balustrade, he had time afforded him for a hurried glance over the almost interminable crowd of heads which rose and sunk as the waving population moved along. The three vast avenues leading up to the palace, from different points of entrance to the town, were crowded to excess: horsemen and carriages slowly made their way along the middle of these wide spaces, and the trees just throwing forth their foliage in the profusion of an early spring, gave an air of bright enjoyment to the scene.—Beyond rose the wood of Sartory, on whose verdant mosses the eye of our hero reposed for a moment, but no more. For at this instant the procession of the royal family, the ministers, and household, and the twelve hundred deputies to the States General, began to move from the palace towards the church, where they went to hear mass, and receive a blessing and offer up prayers, previous to their solemnly assembling on the morrow—all of which were ineffectual for their future good. As the trumpets flourished, and the drums rolled, and the cannons fired, and the people shouted, Cornelius seemed to rise superior to his former state of being. He breathed an atmosphere of sensations unknown to him before; but while he revelled in this new state of excitement, and felt himself as it were identified with these bursts of national delight, a sudden shock threw his memory back upon the desolate contrast which his native land presented to his mind. He had no time however for the indulgence of this mood. The shiftings of thought were too frequent for reflection. The procession began its march: and Cornelius fixed his looks upon the pompous parade of heralds, and ushers, in their gaudy trappings, and supposed that they must have formed the representatives of all the grandeur of the state. The busy murmurings of the crowd soon told him of his error, and he learned from the garrulous by standers all the particulars of the pageant. He saw the noblesse first pass by him, in their splendid apparel of cloth of gold, with white plumes waving proudly, and their brilliance dazzling the beholders—but little importance was attached to the wearers by the people, who had learned to appreciate the true nature of the illustrious obscurity into which this class had fallen. Next came the clergy in their silks and lace and cambric, their white or pink or purple robes failing to command the reverence of the mob, which had been alienated from its former devotion to appearances and forms, not less by the free spirit that was abroad, than by the dissolute conduct and political intrigues of the priesthood. When the deputies of the people advanced, the people seemed to feel their own importance, and shouts of acclamation rose wildly from the throng. The six hundred members of the *tiers-etat* marched past with steady steps and confident looks. Their short black coats and cloaks of the same colour, with their long white muslin cravats, formed a costume, the simplicity of which seemed to give additional dignity to their deportment. But of all the individuals of this order, one was conspicuous on that day—by his haughty bearing, as well as by his long flowing hair, and marked yet forbidding countenance, which possessed the double faculty of attraction and repulsion. It was Mirabeau; his name was shouted by the mob, but they seemed to shrink from him while they applauded; and their voices died away imperfectly, as if he awed while he inspired them.

Cornelius was raised to a pitch of excitement which seemed to have reached its utmost height. He had not been ignorant of the existing events in France. He was well read and well informed on its past and present state, and while he inherited from his father all his principles of attachment to the reigning monarch, his heart bounded within him as he heard the shouts of an emancipated people ringing in his ears. The approach of the household troops recalled him from his flight, for he felt himself to be one of them virtually, though not practically yet; and the anxious but decorous buzz of the crowd was followed by the appearance of the King and the Queen, side by side, followed by his sister Madame Elizabeth, his brothers, and the Duke of Orleans. The strainings of the crowd to get a near view of these chief objects of curiosity forced our hero close to them; for he sturdily preserved the position which chance had given him in the very front of the throng. As the King came near, the enthusiasm of the beholders became tumultuous. The respectful murmur which had whispered his approach, rose by degrees into shouts that might have awoke the echoes of the distant wood. The multitude from behind pressed forward in hopeless and uncalculating efforts to get a glimpse of the monarch, who at this moment stood on the summit of his popularity. The guard and gens-d'armes vainly endeavoured to keep back the crowd. The near presence of the King forbade the least effort to use force against their encroachments, and for some minutes every barrier was broken down, and the march of the procession completely stopped. Cornelius looked on the King with a feeling which at first was awe, but he soon turned from his calm and common-place countenance. He involuntarily compared its heavy and talentless expression with Mirabeau's imperious and audacious glance; but while the instantaneous comparison was glancing across his mind, his eye fell full upon and became rivetted on another person close beside him, the drapery of whose silk robe actually rustled against him as he stood. It was the Queen.

Marie Antoinette was at that period in the very prime of her beauty, in the plenitude of her power, and without question the most interesting woman in Europe. There was something in the unbending energy of her spirit which astonished and enchanted the world. Her vivacity, through which continually burst proofs of deep feeling and a generous mind, softened down the harsh impression which would have been made by her courage, had it been allied to a cold and repulsive manner. Her personal charms were formed to captivate, and her character to secure the admiration of mankind. She had therefore the most devoted servants in all those attached to her person; and those only were her enemies, who were influenced by political causes, or by some prejudice which was hurt by her conduct towards them. No queen had ever greater difficulties to contend with; the sources of which may be shortly enumerated. A despotic and haughty mother, a selfish and intriguing tutor, a neglected education, a husband insensible to her worth, and incapable of bringing it to perfection—unbending political enemies—and a lively, easy disposition. In that short list may be comprised the causes of her faults and her misfortunes. But the knowledge of those evils acted upon those who admired her character as a powerful stimulus for the increase of their attachment. Amongst those was our hero, who had long imbibed from his father the highest opinion of her heart, and the conviction of her purity; and it was with such feelings, called into unpremeditated action by her present position, that he now stood gazing upon her.

The countenance of Marie Antoinette possessed an uncommon union of sweetness and command; and the fashion of dress introduced by her was peculiarly adapted, and perhaps particularly chosen, for its advantageous display. Her hair was on the present occasion, as was usual, dressed in extravagant profusion of height and curls, and her powdered tresses did not want beauty to the eyes accustomed to the disfigurement which a better taste has since abolished. Her high and ample forehead, white and polished, seemed to speak a proud and vigorous mind. Her bright blue eyes were filled with softness and vivacity combined; while the dignified expression of her aquiline nose, and the decisive tone given to her features by her somewhat projecting chin, were blended with the smiles of a mouth, bewitching and seductive beyond description. Her natural complexion was clear and brilliant, and heightened by the use of rouge; while the elegance and tastefulness of her dress accorded well with the mixed character of her beauty. There was never a more perfect union of the queen with the woman; nor an object more powerfully formed to insure the passionate homage of an enthusiast, such as was our hero.* During the favourable, or I should rather say fatal, interval, in which Cornelius thus uninterruptedly gazed upon her personal charms, and figured to himself the perfection of her mental attributes, the fate of his future life was sealed; and, filled with emotions whose nature he dared not attempt to analyze, he felt convinced that an idol was thus raised up for his everlasting adoration.

The interruption given to the procession, and the clamorous applauses of the crowd,

* Those who in the present day would wish to form a notion of the truth of this sketch, must consult the celebrated portrait by Madame Le Brun, now in the Palace of St. Cloud, and a small bust in Sevres China, which stands in the *Foyer* of the Salle de Spectacle in the Palace of Versailles, and of which I do not know any duplicate.

seemed for an instant to ruffle the calmness of the King, for he looked round him hurriedly and even wistfully, as if he suspected something sinister, or wished to assure himself that all was right. The expression of the Queen's countenance was also changed, but it was into one of haughty firmness, the natural effect of imagined danger on the faces of the brave. She stood steadily, holding the King's arm with a grasp that seemed meant to give not demand security. But there was really nothing to apprehend: the irruption of the crowd into the regulated limits of the procession proceeded purely from their over-zealous attachment to the King, and the air resounded with his name. *Vive le Roi!* was shouted almost stunningly into his ears; while only a few faint voices joined, *et la Reine!* Cornelius heard the clamour, but his mind was too much absorbed to mark the distinction which was evidently observed—painfully and proudly—by the Queen. Her face shewed a dignified indifference of the popular voice—a fatal and deep-rooted error in her character. The negative dispraise, conveyed by the slight mention of her name, produced no further positive effect upon her; but just when the obstruction was removed and the procession resuming its march, a ruffianly fellow, who stood close to our hero, interrupted the somewhat increasing cry of "Long live the King and the Queen!" by bawling out "No, no, the King and the Duke of Orleans!" At this brutal insult the whole soul of the indignant Queen seemed to mount into her eyes. She threw a glance of reproachful contempt upon the ruffian, which, while it flushed by Cornelius, seemed half conveyed to him. In the roused state of his feelings at the moment he knew not what he did, but the natural impulse of his mind burst forth in a loud shout of "*Vive la Reine! Vive la Reine!*" he accompanied the cry by corresponding gestures of enthusiasm; and the whole surrounding concourse following the impulse thus given, burst into a general chorus of the inspiring exclamation.

The Queen seemed electrically affected by the sudden change. Her eyes were suffused in tears—her forehead was covered with a glow of delight. Her lips quivered with emotion—and as she moved on with majestic step, she gracefully waved her hand to those around her, as she inclined her head and threw an eloquent smile towards our hero, whose animated interference she had minutely observed. The smile sank deep into his breast. He trembled from head to foot with excess of rapture, his eyes swam, and almost involuntarily he sunk on one knee, bowing down his head and stretching forth his arms as if to an object of religious homage. When the rush of the crowd forced him to rise up, a confused mass of guards and followers met his eye.

He gazed after the line of the procession, but he could distinguish nothing of her whom he sought. But his mind was filled with her, and he needed not her actual presence as an inspiration to his transported feelings. Oppressed by the crowd, he burst away from its obstruction; and reckless of his course, he wandered in the direction of the palace gardens. Passing through the court-yard, which was by this time free for the public, he walked hastily along, close by the chapel, without observing its architecture, or its stained glass windows, which formed a contrast, striking enough to common passers-by, with the old tasteless brick-work and gilding of the front face of the narrow-casemented low-roofed residence of the French King. Cornelius stepped through the side portico and paced the broad and gravelled way, without observing aught around him, until he reached the extremity of the terrace in front, and found himself on the first of the flights of broad steps, which lead down to the *Tapis vert*, the *bosquets*, and the park. His attention was arrested for an instant, and all his contemplations interrupted, by the extent and splendour of the scene. The masses of wood, the broad sheets of water, the wide walks, the numerous statues, the flowers and shrubs were all opened on his view, as if by magic. He turned round, and the whole extent of the façade of the royal structure, stretching out to the right and left, in all its vastness and splendour, seemed as if suddenly conjured up by some enchanter's wand.

This burst of magnificence was quite in unison with the "thick coming fancies," which filled the imagination of our hero. Such a palace and such a park, seemed suited to the one being who occupied his thoughts, and whatever he gazed on was seen through the medium of the adoration, which that being had so suddenly, but so irrevocably inspired. He moved along in a state of rapt abstraction, and saw every thing as it were enfolded in a veil of unreal excitement.

The throng from the streets and the church now began to pour into the park, and the water-works commenced their play. Discharges of artillery announced the return of the procession to the palace, and the moving thousands of spectators scattered in fluttering gaudiness through the parterres, lawns, and walks. The woods were alive with joyous groups which sported in the green places. The glittering trappings of the military mixed with the varied coloured robes of innumerable fair forms. The waters from a hundred fountains rose towards the sky, caught the iris-forming sunbeams, which sported in a halo around each liquid column, and then fell in sparkling mists upon the bosom of the lakes. The miniature vessels had their sails outspread and swam at random on the water, while the swans swelled out their plumage, and seemed to float in proud rivalry of these artificial intruders. Music from many stations was sounding in the breeze; and green meadows, in the distance, contrasted with the mellower tints of the woods, till they were lost at the foot of a mass of fleecy clouds, which rose on the horizon in the fantastic semblance of a snow-covered mountain chain.

While Cornelius ranged this scene of fairy land, he had no disposition for its critical examination. He could not analyze the magnificent display, nor separate its masses of grand effect, to cavil at clipped trees, straight walks, or formal flower plots. He wandered about without plan from avenue to avenue, through those delicious bosquets profusely planted in the park, and decorated each with some new ornament. In spite of his reveries he could not pass by without noticing the beautiful spot called the Baths of Apollo, where the marble figure of the god, sculptured into a resemblance of Louis XIV. with four nymphs, likenesses of the vain-glorious monarch's mistresses, all rest in a group of exquisite design, under the vault of rock-work, artificially massed in rivalry of nature's most romantic scenes; while the gush of waters from above flows down through overhanging shrubs and flowers, and after bathing the feet of the horses of the sun, which are tended by satyrs below, falls into an irregular grass-edged basin that can be scarcely believed the formation of art. Another of those tree-embosomed creations of pure taste which roused our hero's attention was the circular colonnade, surrounding the group which represents the Rape of Proserpine. To this place he was attracted by the sounds of music, and in the centre of the open space he observed the musicians,—while the slightly elevated terrace and the steps leading to it were thronged with listeners, who walked through the double row of pillars, each one of a kind of marble different from its fellows,—and heard the strains of music mix with the murmurs of the fairy fountains, which fell into broad basins in each interval between the columns.

While our hero thus listlessly loitered along, the noiseless wings of Evening began to throw their shadow across the scene, and the sun flung his farewell beams around him as he sunk slowly behind the woods; the clouds were reflected in the lakes; and the countless windows of the palace glowed with the gorgeous mixtures of gold and crimson hues. These signs of the close of day acted as usual upon the sensitive caution of a French crowd, and the assembled multitude hastily broke away, to take refuge in the heated *fumes* of the *Cafés* from the terrors of the delicious twilight air. Cornelius almost instinctively approached the palace—for there was but little of calculation in the notion that stole across his mind that he might again catch a view of the Queen. As he crossed the *Tapis vert*, a large grass-plat which stretches down to the border of the lake, and listened to the gushing melody of the nightingales, he was aroused by sounds of tumult proceeding from one of the close alleys, and as he looked for explanation, a crowd approached him, composed of the straggling remains of idle company and several of the guardian officers of the park. The latter were hustling along a man who struggled violently, and who raised such a dust around him as to prevent our hero from distinguishing his features or dress, and whose screams were almost stifled by the threats and execrations of those who held him, and the loud bursts of laughter of the spectators. Cornelius, prompted by a mixed impulse of curiosity and hatred of any thing that savoured of oppression, pressed forward, and as he mingled with the throng, plainly distinguished the hoarse cries of Bryan Mulcahie, who called aloud on his master, "Master Cornalius, Master Cornalius! where are you, where are you? let me go, you villains —where are you, where are you? oh you murthering thieves, do you want to choak me? and is it for this that I followed you to be murthered and robbed this way? Master Cornalius, Master Cornalius!"

The close of this sentence, which was uttered at the very top of poor Bryan's half cracked voice, was answered by a renewed volley of oaths from the guards, and roars of laughter from the crowd. Cornelius could with difficulty restrain his desire of rushing to the rescue of his hapless follower; but he was resolved to ascertain the nature of Bryan's offence before he committed himself by an inconsiderate interference. He therefore enquired of one of the by-standers, and learned that the culprit having entered the gardens, had begun roaring forth lustily in his barbarous English dialect, apparently for some companion whom he sought; that he instantly attracted the observation of the crowd, many of whom fled from him, supposing him some maniac; but the majority amused themselves by laughing at his grotesque costume and conduct, which so irritated Bryan, that he commenced a fierce attack upon those nearest to him, on which the guards interfered, and Bryan finding himself overpowered, had attempted an escape, and bounding across various flower plots and other sacred places, was at last seized in the violated sanctuary of one of the queen's own arbours. At this detail Cornelius was somewhat puzzled how to act, but he thought it most wise to let the law of the place take its course, which he supposed would most naturally lead the prisoner to the guard house. He therefore accompanied the group, taking great care to conceal himself from the roaring Bryan. The guards led along towards the front terrace, and while they began to drag the prisoner up the steps, he made the most resolute struggles, taking a fresh position of defence on every flight, and kicking with his nail-embossed shoes against his conductors, whose shins must have been as hard as the marble they trod on, not to have shewn bruises as varied as its veins. Showers of blows from the thin canes, and scratches from the open hands of the unscientific Frenchmen assailed poor Bryan; and Cornelius, unable longer to resist his feelings, was bursting through the crowd to assist him, when a priest of tall and gaunt figure, about forty-five years of age, attracted by the cries of the sufferer, threw himself before him and the guards, and seizing the two who throttled Bryan, one in each of his powerful hands, he shook them from their hold; while Bryan finding himself free, immediately sprung at them and struck them right and left, until their defenceless faces streamed with blood. The beholders, amazed and somewhat shocked at this contest, left the field open to the operation of the priest, who, while he shook the terrified guards with gigantic force, poured out on them his upbraidings in stentorian tones, for their cowardly treatment of a defenceless foreigner.

"Oh! ye thieving spalpeens!" cried Bryan, redoubling his blows.

"Be aisy, my lad," interrupted the priest. "Let them alone and lave them to me; I'm Father O'Collogan, late of the Irish Brigade; so don't be afeard of any harm coming to you; I'll take care of you, body and soul both."

"Och! then long life to your reverence, if you be an Irishman, for I did not think there was another in it, barring Master Cornalius and myself—and I'm sartain sure these villains have murthered him."

Here the guards, with humble mien, but vociferous protestations, accused Bryan, and claimed him as their prisoner.

"Don't believe a word they say, your reverence," interrupted Bryan; "it's all lies from top to bottom. I did nothing at all at all, but look for Master Cornalius, and gave a tap or two to the fellows that made faces at me, and broke an old flower pot when the thieves runned after me."

The guards here put in a rejoinder, swearing lustily that all Bryan's asseverations were false; (although they no more understood him than he did them) and accusing him of having offended against the laws of good breeding, by interrupting the harmony of the place with his barbarous and brutal exclamations, knocking down a hair-dresser and a dancing-master who smiled at his extravagance, tearing up with his hoofs many most precious flowers, and rushing like a wild boar into the sacred recesses of the queen's favourite bosquet.

"It's all a lie, all a lie!" roared Bryan during this detail; "I was only looking for Master Cornalius."

Father O'Collogan assured the guards they should have every satisfaction, and while the whole party advanced in the direction of the palace, to reach the wing where the ranger of the park was to be found, he turned to Bryan, and demanded what he meant by the frequent mention of "Master Cornelius."

"Main, your reverence? why I main that I was looking for Master Cornalius, my master, the son of the ould master, Major ——, of the castle, that's all, your reverence."

"What is it you're after telling me?" asked the Priest sternly: "do you want to persuade me that Cornelius, the son of my friend the Major, would be here in Versailles without coming to see me? I believe you're a bit of a big blackguard, and a liar into the bargain."

"It's God's truth I tell you, saving your reverence's presence," blubbered Bryan, unable longer to restrain his tears, "and I'm as innocent as the babe unborn."

"Where is your master then?" asked the priest.

"I dunna where the divil he is, plase your honour, if these villains hav'n't murthered him, as they thought to do me." A burst of grief followed this speech.

"If you're telling truth," cried Father O'Collogan, "I'll find him out for you, dead or alive, never fear that."

Cornelius, who attentively listened to this colloquy, was now on the point of advancing to introduce himself to Father O'Collogan, in hopes of terminating the affair; when the whole party, which had advanced close up to the palace in its way towards the court yard, was stopped by a servant in the royal livery, who advanced quickly from beside a group of ladies and gentlemen, who were walking immediately in front of the open windows. The domestic announced himself as a forerunner of a chamberlain, sent by the queen herself, who was in the group just mentioned, and who, having observed the prominent figure of the priest in this crowd, was curious to know the particulars of what was passing. While Father O'Collogan put his ruffled cassock and band in order, and by the interference of his bony fingers rather increased than rectified the confusion of his powdered curls, and while the guards decorously wiped away from their faces the marks of Bryan's sanguinary attacks, the chamberlain aforesaid, in full dress, advanced with courtier-like and mincing steps, and holding his sword and hat gracefully under one arm, he shook perfumes from his cambric handkerchief, as he enquired into the nature of this tumultuous proceeding, under the very windows of the palace.

Father O'Collogan began most fluently and energetically to explain the affair, advocating poor Bryan's cause, and pronouncing him entitled to a full pardon on the score of his ignorance of French etiquette, and his slight experience in the intercourse of civilized society. But before the priest's harangue had nearly come to a close, the queen and her attendants had advanced quite close, and Marie Antoinette herself, with that condescending grace, which, had she been queen of England would have enthroned her in the people's hearts, but which the French were incapable of appreciating, instantly entered into the enquiry, and learned from the mouth of the undaunted priest the whole circumstances of the case. As Cornelius stood gazing upon her, he forgot every thing but her, and the enquiry was carried on unattended to by him. He thought that fate seemed to have thus thrown him into the presence of the queen, twice in one day, as if to sanction the adoration with which he viewed her; and she appeared to him now, in her undress, and freed from the splendid but formal trappings of the morning, a thousand times more beautiful than she had been then. Having attentively listened to Father O'Collogan's harangue in explanation of Bryan's situation relative to our hero, she recommended the dismissal of the prisoner, under the priest's safe convoy; and telling the guards to be satisfied, she ended by expressing a hope that the young Garde-du-Corps would be soon found to come forward, to enter on his own duties, and keep his servant within the bounds of his.

Cornelius hearing these concluding words, felt irresistibly impelled to avow himself, and advancing from the crowd, he bent forward, and declared that he was the master of the offender, for whose future propriety he vouched; at the same time professing his gratitude for her majesty's gracious interference. The queen instantly recognised our hero. She bowed and smiled—little imagining the fatal consequences of the smile on him, into whose heart it found immediate entrance.

"It is well," said the queen, turning away; and she added to her beautiful companion, the Princess Lamballe, "this young Irishman will not disgrace the ranks of the Gardes-du-Corps."

"He is superb," replied the princess, "and worthy to serve such a mistress."

"It's him! it's him! sure enough," exclaimed

Bryan, the moment he caught sight of our hero.—"Och, Master Cornalius, how could you sarve me such a turn? Did you ait any thing? The devil a morsel entered your mouth, I'll be bound for it, since breakfast, and it's past seven o'clock. For the love of Jasus, come home, and get some dinner, for I'm starving alive wid the exercise I took thumping these French thieves here: the devil's the lie in it.—Here's Father O'Collogan, Master Cornalius, he'll tell you all about it if you don't believe me."

Upon this introduction, our hero and his father's old friend and companion commenced their personal acquaintance: Cornelius excused himself from the reproaches of the good priest, by telling him the circumstances of his recent arrival, and his reasons for avoiding an instantaneous intrusion; and Father O'Collogan proposing to accompany him to his barracks, to receive his father's letter, and to pass the remainder of the evening with him, they set out together for Cornelius's quarters, close followed by Bryan, who defended the impatience which brought him out in search of his master, and was pursued by a long train of followers, who could not resist the attraction of a last view of the wild Irishman.

The evening passed quickly, to the apprehension of the worthy priest, who talked fluently to Cornelius on a thousand topics, past, present, and future, made numberless enquiries for his old companions, related various anecdotes of their former intercourse, and touched deeply on our hero's duties in his new station, and on the political aspect of the times. Cornelius, on his part, thought the evening would never end. The garrulity of his companion, and the loud snoring of Bryan, who by his master's orders went to his early bed, in a nook outside the anti-room, were equally annoying. His mind, full of one great object, was harassed by the comparatively petty subjects which Father O'Collogan touched on so abundantly. It was not till the latter mentioned the queen, that his hitherto reluctant listener could even assume an interest in his remarks; but when her name and situation became the topic, he gave an intense attention to all that was said.

"Aye," said the priest solemnly, "aye, and this beautiful crature of a queen, who might be thought, from her condescension and goodness, to be an angel, even she will suffer, I'll warrant it, from these very States General. It's hard to say what one must expect in the time that's before us; but take my word for it, the poor thing has reason to look with a heavy heart and heavy eye, on what's coming to pass.

'*Le tems present est gros de l'Avenir.*'—

To-day to our sorrow
'S with child of to-morrow,

as the poet says, and a devil of a troublesome child that same morrow will be, I'm sore afeard."

"I hope, my dear Sir," said Cornelius, "that your forebodings are unfounded, and that you see things too much in the shade. Surely every appearance of this day promises happiness and greatness to the country, the king and the queen."

"Don't be too sure of that, my dear boy," replied the priest; "you don't know the ill will that's working against her at any rate. Every thing bad, I tell you once more, is to be expected from these States General, and the turn the public mind is taking. We may say with Horace

'Grave virus munditias pellet;'

That is, putting it in the future,

The plague spreads, and soon will ate
Each healthy portion of the state.

"Why it's even reported about the palace, that at the procession this very day, a creature of that bad madman, the Duke of Orleans, insulted her majesty grossly, and was even going to strike her, till he was knocked down by a young Englishman, or a young Irishman may be; for that's more like."

"It is false, my good Sir," exclaimed Cornelius; "no one could be monster enongh to dream of, much less attempt such an outrage."

"And how do you know that?" asked the priest quickly.

"Because I was there, on the spot.—Because in fact, I was—I was—."

"You were the young foreigner that knocked the fellow down," interrupted Father O'Collogan; "I see it all with half an eye.—It was you then! Oh, the blood of my friend the Major is boiling in your fine full veins! You knocked him down, the thief!"

"No, my dear Sir," protested Cornelius, "no such thing I assure you."—

"Yes, but you did though—I know better nor you.—Don't deny it—never be ashamed of a good action. It was your bounden duty as a christian.—Where did you hit him, tell me?"

Before our hero could put another negative on the priest's assertion, a knock at the door interrupted the discussion, and the adjutant of the troop to which Cornelius was appointed, entered with a message from the Colonel, who had just returned from the queen's private party, intimating that as a complete muster of the troop would be required to attend the king on the morrow, for the opening of the States General, he expected that Cornelius would be ready to follow the parade as a supernumerary. The new recruit expressed his readiness to obey, but at the same time lamented his want of a suit of uniform, as well as his total ignorance of manœuvres and parade discipline. "All that I will take upon myself," replied the adjutant: "one of your brother guardsmen has promised to lend you a suit which will fit you, and I shall expect nothing from you, but to follow the march of the troop without joining in its movements."

After these words the adjutant was retiring, when Father O'Collogan addressed him; and it will be recollected by my readers, that the priest spoke French in a different style from English.

"Yes yes, adjutant, depend upon it he shall attend. I see the whole matter clearly. The queen has desired the colonel to have him present."—

"Oh, Monsieur l'Abbé!" exclaimed the adjutant.

"For God's sake, my dear Sir!" cried Cornelius.

"Never mind, gentlemen, I tell you both she did—I know the way of the sex, and I know the way of the queen—and she is right to like to have before her eyes this fine young fellow, Mr. Adjutant, that knocked down the scoundrel who insulted her this morning at the procession."

"Why, is this indeed the gentleman?" demanded the adjutant anxiously.

"To be sure it is," reiterated the priest; and before Cornelius could say a word more in denial, the adjutant precipitately retired, and in a few minutes returned with above a dozen of the guards, whom he brought back with him to introduce to the gallant comrade, who had already signalized himself as the champion of their idolized mistress. Denial and protestation were useless on the part of our hero, and asseveration was not wanted, though freely offered, on the part of the priest, to robe him in a reputation which we can scarcely call unmerited. In an hour Cornelius's imagined conduct was bruited through the barracks; and before the parade time next morning, almost all the royalist population of Versailles had got the story, and his name in their mouths. He was thus already a marked man.

CHAPTER VI.

The following day, the 5th of May, 1789, was one of those delusive epochs in the calendar of a kingdom's fate, whose arrival is hailed by the world with enthusiasm proportioned to the good it promises, and which is looked back on with sentiments of profound contempt for the shallow calculations of mankind. At that period France stood immensely high in the scale of national greatness. Her conduct was the polar star of European guidance; and it depended on her to secure the liberties of the world by her moderation, as she had up to that moment advanced them by her firmness. At the assembling of the States General, all Europe was imbued with the spirit of freedom, and even its most powerful despots, Catherine, Frederick, and Joseph, had either promulgated or patronised liberal opinions, and were ready to adopt the course of constitutional independence which seemed to be preparing in France. But all the bright views of philanthropy were deceived, and its justified hopes destroyed, by the inebriate fury of a faction, and the national degradation of the mass. Liberty was strangled in her cradle; and the phantom fiend which sprung up in her place, betrayed its spuriousness by the rapidity of its growth, and terrified the world by the giant strides which trampled down the fresh-springing flowers of genuine freedom.

It cannot be doubted that Louis XVI. participated fully in the general wish for the reformation of abuses, and the establishment of a constitution. His great object was to see his subjects contented, even at the expense of his prerogative. But it is as certain, that Marie Antoinette had different notions. She wished the people well, but she would have preserved the power of making them so; of retailing to them individually their indulgences at her pleasure;—the wholesale happiness to be given to them, by deductions from her own or her husband's privileges, was not consistent with her views. Cradled in despotism, and fostered by flattery, she had not force of mind sufficient to see the value, or the necessity of sacrifices. She possessed a vigorous character rather than a strong intellect; and while the king, from his softness, would yield one by one, the powers which he inherited, she clung to each with a tenacity, which, contrasted with his weakness, made him appear contemptible, and herself odious, in the eyes of the people. But these results of their unsympathising dispositions, were not developed till after the period before us. When the States General met together, the king was most popular, and the queen not hated.

The spectacle of that day was the finest that had been witnessed in France for ages. Louis was seated on his throne glittering in gold and jewels, the princes of the blood around him; the queen, the princesses, and the ladies of the court, in magnificent dresses, gracing the side galleries of the hall, and its body filled with the nobles, the clergy, and the representatives of the people; altogether forming a rare combination of outward splendour and moral greatness. The speech of the king was well composed, well delivered, and enthusiastically received. But Cornelius, who by the special favour of his colonel, was placed so as to have a full view of this remarkable assembly, paid but little regard to the oration of the king or the ministers. His mind was absorbed in the contemplation of the queen, who sat silently, and as our hero thought sadly, looking down on the assembled elements, and on many of the agents of her after misery. Whether a boding of ill, or a sense of degradation acted on her then, it would be hard to say; but we can scarcely think of her in the solitude of her recorded emotion on that day of general joy, without fancying her to have had some prophetic glance into the horrid futurity of her fate. Cornelius thought of the priest's prognostications, and he almost shuddered as he gazed on the grandeur around him. He followed the royal family to the palace, with the troop which escorted them, and urged by the ardour of his feelings, and the intuitive desire to gain one glance of recognition, he pressed close to the carriage from which the queen descended; but she had no thoughts for him, or the many devoted followers who surrounded her that day. Who may say what occupied her mind?

As Cornelius wound slowly back to his barracks in the rear of the guard, he felt a depression of spirits unexperienced ever until then. The day before that very morning, as well as during the sleepless night that intervened, he had known a buoyancy of heart, of a nature undefinable and vague; but perhaps more delightful than more positive sensations. These were the earliest hours of that one deep attachment, which almost all men experience—so unlike the fugitive visitings of common love—when the heart of the enthusiast acknowledges an impression, which it is unable to comprehend, and never may forget. The delicious reveries of those few hours, in which the mind cannot think, nor the eyes close,—when appetite is dead, and every thing a dreamy enchantment—are only broken by some painful sympathy with her who gave them birth; and the chain of visioned abstractions is snapped by some touch of actual feeling, which she alone can create.

Cornelius paced his room that evening with an air of deep depression. He appeared to himself to have suddenly started from the delusions of sleep, and he entered on the task of self-examination with a degree of intense pain. He was amazed and shocked, as he called up in review the sensations of the last twenty-four hours. He wished to doubt the reality of his feelings, for he shrunk back, and felt his face glow, when the remembrance of his daring thoughts was raised in evidence to his mind. The presumption of his aspirations, even to be noticed or known by the queen of France, appeared to him to merit contempt and punishment. He felt as if the whole world had pierced the secret, which he was afraid to acknowledge to himself. He sank on a chair, and covered his face with his hands, as he reflected in shame on the boldness with which he had gazed at, followed, and even spoken to her. He had heard in conversation amongst the guards that morning, of a gentleman who at that moment wandered about Versailles, harmlessly mad from love of the queen. As the thought of this man returned upon Cornelius, he sprang from his seat, and felt his heart's blood run chill—for he feared that *his* senses too might have wandered, which alone might account for his audacious thoughts. But all the struggles of forced reasoning with an involuntary passion ended, as is usual, in the latter acquiring fresh force from every effort to suppress it. Cornelius, as his first emotion of self-reproach subsided, became convinced that though he ought not to imagine the probability of his loving the queen, he was bound in duty as well as inclination to be devoted to her wholly. And proud in the conviction that he had thus, in its early stage, shaken off the witchery that was stealing on his heart, he added one to the list of those self-deceivers, who believe reason to be more powerful than passion.

I have stated that our hero had already become a marked man, through the positive misconception of the part he acted at the procession. Every hour increased his notoriety; for Father O'Collogan, in the true spirit of Irish friendship, talked unceasingly in his praise, and spread a hundred innocent untruths about him, which had their birth in the inventive fertility of the good priest's imagination. Amongst other things he told every body that "the queen, and small blame to her, sweet soul that she was, had taken a powerful fancy to the handsome young Irishman, as soon as ever she saw him knock down the fellow that was going to strike her; that she had come out on the terrace on purpose to look at him that evening, and natural enough it was; that she had made the colonel insist on his joining the parade the next morning, and for sure had looked more at, and thought more about him, than about the States General—fine a sight as it was."

All these absurd exaggerations came quite natural to Father O'Collogan. He believed every word of them, and meant any thing but evil to the queen. He thought nothing was more natural or more innocent, and therefore more certain, than her strong partiality for our hero—and all the rest of his conclusions followed in course. And it was thus unfortunately that many of the best friends of Marie Antoinette struck death blows to her reputation, which they would have died to uphold. Every enemy, every scandal-monger, every babbler of the town, caught each absurd report, and echoed it around; and, amongst others equally false, it was now loudly asserted that she had formed a violent liking to the young Irishman; and the vile fancies of the public set no bounds to this imagined attachment.

Cornelius was most unconsciously an object of general observation. He became a subject for the envy, and of course the enmity of many of his brother guardsmen; and to the avowed enemies of the queen, who every day increased even among the military, he was a noted mark for injury or insult, whenever occasion might serve. He inadvertently added to the calumnies which were abroad, by the reserved deportment at all times natural to him, but which was now increased from the state of the feeling by which he was absorbed. All this was set down to pride; and his late solitary walks in the park were attributed to other and more positive causes.

A month passed over in this manner. Cornelius, devoting himself with great ardour to the routine of his military instruction, was getting quickly through the early duties of a recruit; and when he walked the streets, or rode to the exercise ground, in his suit of handsome blue uniform, or when he attended at the evening parties to which he was invited in the palace or the town, in his full-dress coat richly laced with gold, with scarlet velvet breeches and silk stockings, he was allowed to be among the most striking of the handsome youths who at that time adorned the court of Versailles. He felt an elevation of spirit, from the noble incitement which urged him on, that raised his manners to a level with his mind; and he bore in his deportment the marks of a consciousness of some dignified motive of thought and action. He sometimes saw the queen, during her promenades, or when he happened to be on duty at the palace; and labouring to convince himself that he had stifled the first symptoms of a passion which he dared not indulge, he attributed to respectful zeal the throbbings of the heart, and swimming of the brain which oppressed him whenever she appeared. In his letters to his father he spoke with delight of his situation; touched slightly on public affairs, but never mentioned the queen. Neither did he speak of her in his intercourse with his comrades, or in society. But to Father O'Collogan he freely talked of his devotion to her cause, of his admiration of her conduct, and with a warmth encouraged by the priest's continual assurances that he had found favour in the sight of his royal mistress; assurances which, while they were at the moment actually painful to our hero, worked their deep effect on his mind, and fostered the ambitious fervour of his unconfessed attachment.

During all this time poor Bryan felt himself very ill at ease. The fine laced livery and cocked hat in which he was decked sat ungracefully upon him, as he thought, and his inability to express his grievances was worse than the grievances themselves. A butt for the unceasing pranks and pleasantries of the soldier-servant granted to Cornelius, he had little consolation. The military character of his master and his abstracted mien filled him with an increasing awe that threw him out of the way of common confidence, and his only relief was his occasional confessions to Father O'Collogan. He used to talk to him about home, and "the ould master," and his "poor mother," and "the castle" and Ireland—until the good nature and patriotism of the warm-hearted priest would overflow in streams of the purest benevolence. As an employment to Bryan, whose only actual occupation was the cleaning of his master's horse, Father O'Collogan recommended the study of the French language. Bryan faithfully promised, and worked hard to pick up a word here and there, and his progress may be judged of, from his having told his master at the end of a month, that "he knew very well how to ax *for* a bit and a sup, *for dillo* was water, and *mungey* meant aiting."

Among the acquaintances formed by Cornelius, in the first days of his arrival at Versailles, was a young man of about his own age, named Armand. This youth was well known as the protegé of the queen, who had picked him up a child in one of her drives, adopted him with the consent of his parents, who were poor cottagers, and had had him reared and educated with all the indulgence and luxury common to the children of persons of rank. From these circumstances he was known among the people of Versailles by the nickname of *Le Marquis de Rencontre.* He was handsome and intelligent, but he had a good deal of the arrogance of people of low birth raised by no merit of their own to a high station in society: and this was increased, as it ever is, by the rankling feeling of the contempt attached to him by his high born associates; which forced him to an insolence of demeanour, as the only chance of preserving his artificial level. He had also a dash of the libertine about him—an unsteadiness of principle and opinion—which evidently shewed that he had no moral feeling strong enough to keep him in the right course. Cornelius soon perceived all these points in his character, and he was, perhaps, the last associate our hero would have chosen, had it not been from that involuntary attraction which led him towards every thing that harmonized with his devotion, which was rapidly becoming idolatry. He calculated on Armand's attachment to the queen, and on the chances which might arise from an intimacy with him for his seeing her in less formal circumstances than his public duty permitted. In these views Cornelius was quite successful, for he not only procured, by means of his new acquaintance, facilities for private entrance into the palace and the gardens of the Trianons, but he had continued occasions of hearing of the queen, in all her domestic pursuits; and he even gained so far on the good will of Armand, as to get from him a small portion of a lock of her hair taken from some fixed in the setting behind a miniature, which his royal patroness had presented to him on one of her fête days, as the most affectionate token of her regard.

Provided with this treasure, Cornelius felt himself possessed of an amulet, not against the evil chances of fate, but against what they too commonly arise from, the evil conduct of men. With the lock of her hair on his heart, and her image ever in his mind, he was satisfied that he could not possibly commit an unworthy action; for he felt like all those who imagine the presence of a revered object, as if there was something approaching the holiness of religious fervour in these sentiments, which in raising him to this perpetually fancied communion, seemed to lift him high above the grosser failings of humanity. One evening in the month of June, as he walked with Armand in the neighbourhood of the Trianons, the oppressive heat of the weather forced them to take shelter in one of those little pleasure gardens, some of which are to be found even now on the outskirts of the park. At that period, when the population of Versailles was five times its present amount, and the constant presence of a large military force added gaiety to the neighbourhood, those little *guinguettes* were the scenes of continual revelry, dancing and enjoyment. On the evening in question, the one in which Armand and Cornelius sheltered themselves was crowded to excess, every arbour was occupied by some party, sipping their lemonade, or orgeat and water; while the dancing ground was occupied by a group who tripped it rather gracefully than gaily, to the sound of a good orchestra elevated among the branches of some acacias, whose white blossoms came down with every breeze in showers of fragrance on the floor.

The companions looked in vain for a seat, and were obliged to content themselves by standing under the shade, and observing the light movements of the dancers, who seemed insensible to the heat which had so much incommoded them. While they gazed, and exchanged their passing observations, they remarked that they were in their turn observed. A group, consisting of three or four officers of a regiment of chasseurs, then quartered at the cavalry barracks at Sevres, and as many more of the National Guard of Versailles, sat drinking in one of the arbours. Their conversation was boisterous, and every word bore directly or indirectly a political meaning. They talked loudly of the discussions at this time beginning to manifest themselves in the States General, and of the contests inevitably about to arise between the people and the throne. They next spoke of the king in terms of insolent allusion—and from that topic they came to the queen. Cornelius and Armand had hitherto listened with comparative indifference, but now they felt all their attention aroused. It was quite evident that the conversation was directed at them. Armand's person was well known, and the uniform of Cornelius made him at once conspicuous, but he too was more particularly recognised as the *Garde-du-Corps*, respecting whom such calumnies were afloat. Snatches of popular songs were sung by the party, bearing upon the minions of the court and its servile hirelings. Loose hints were flung at random, and coarse jests went round, all pointed at our hero and his companion. The dance ceased, and all this became evident to the company. Many seemed to participate in the sentiments of the insulting bravos, and the rest of the party were either indifferent or unobserving as to what was passing.

From the moment that these proceedings took a personal turn, but still more when they seemed connected with the queen, Cornelius felt rooted to the spot by the intense desire of marking some word or phrase on which he could decidedly fix; but the feeling of profound respect always mingled with his thoughts of her, made him shrink from any violence which might compromise her name. He therefore waited with all the outward calmness which his boiling indignation allowed him to assume; and he also considered it a point of duty to leave the first notice of what passed to Armand, in right of his more prominent situation in society, and more particularly from the relation in which he stood towards the queen. But Armand, to his great amaze, shewed no desire to interfere. He seemed, on the contrary, as if he wished to assume a want of consciousness of any thing offensive, and after some casual remarks in an embarrassed air, he proposed to Cornelius that they should retire from the place.

"What!" cried the latter, "would you go, and leave these bullying ruffians to assert that we fled from their insults?"

"Come away, my dear friend," replied the other; "recollect how delicately I am placed. Were I to step forward as the champion of the queen, I should have a dozen duels on my hands —for heaven's sake come."

"Is it thus you argue, Armand?" said Cornelius. "You astonish me! can such considerations make you submit to indignities offered to her name?"

"Why no, not exactly," said his companion in a half-whisper, and at the same time leading Cornelius by the arm; "but you know a brawl on her account might do her more injury than service at this crisis—so do, my friend, come quietly away."

Cornelius yielded slowly to the movement which led him along, but was just framing a reply to prove the disgrace of a retreat, when one of the hostile party shouted loudly—

"I told you so, my comrades. There they go, sneaking away, beaten from the field without a blow!—worthy the minions of the modern Messalina! Victory, victory!"

"By heavens, this is too bad!" exclaimed Cornelius, disengaging his arm from the grasp of Armand.

"Come on, come on," cried the latter, "we shall be murdered else!"

"Let us die then," replied our hero, "sooner than brook these atrocious insults!" and with these words, he burst from the renewed hold of his companion, and stalked up to the table at which the bravos sat.

"Which of this company," demanded he sternly, "dared to utter those calumnious epithets?"

"All, all," cried they with one voice, and rising from their seats.—"We all uttered them."

"And all repeat them," said one of the national guard.

"Then you are all liars and traitors," exclaimed Cornelius," "and I stand here to make good my words."

He instantly drew his sword, and stepped back a pace, to put himself in a posture of defence. They quickly followed his movement, and half-a dozen sabres glittered at once before him.

The whole party rushed forward, and in the unpremeditated fury of the moment, they would have cut their opponent in pieces, had not one of the chasseurs, a huge fellow of fierce aspect, with immense mustachios curling below his chin, thrown himself between our hero and his assailants.

"Stand back, stand back, comrades!" cried he in an authoritative voice,—"would you fall on a single man? For shame—for shame! no, he must choose amongst us. Give him fair play, and let him meet his death honorably to us all!"

"Down with him!" cried some; "let him choose then," said others;—"which of us will you take?" "Give me the pleasure of cutting your throat!" "It was I that uttered the words, make haste, Minion!" and such phrases were uttered all at once by the party.

"Since I must choose amongst you then," said our hero, "I shall take him with the long mustachios. He seems less a ruffian than the rest."

"Cut him in pieces!" vociferated the others, and they rushed closer towards him, when the chasseur once more threw himself between them, and cried out, "Hold every one! he has chosen me, and sealed his own fate. He shall die by my hand. Let no one dare to touch him; he belongs to me alone!"

"Come on then, come on!" exclaimed Cornelius. "Not so, my friend," replied the chasseur, calmly. "It must not be said that you had foul play, you are alone here."

"Alone!" cried Cornelius, looking round, and for the first time observing that he was abandoned by Armand; "no matter, come on!"

"No, Sir," said the chasseur, "not now certainly. But in two hours hence the moon will be up. We shall have better light than now, and less company. Go look for a friend, but beware of *the Marquis*. I shall expect you yonder,—there, under the walls of the Menagerie.

You have no time to lose," added he, "and here is my card, that you may know whom to ask for if the moon be overcast."

"I shall be punctual," said Cornelius, "and am glad to have to deal with a man of honor." And pulling out one of his own cards in exchange for that which he took, he walked away, sheathing his sword, and followed by glances of respect and admiration from the crowd.

As he moved briskly on towards the town, by the shortest path leading through the park, his mind was in a state of high effervescence. A confusion of thoughts arose, but uppermost was the wish for vengeance on the daring slanderers of the queen.

"Yes, she shall be revenged, by heavens!" cried he to himself, clenching his fist and raising it towards heaven. Just as he uttered the spontaneous exclamation, something rustled in the grove beside him, and as he clapped his hand to his sword, Armand jumped out on the path.

"Good God, it is you, then!" cried he; "you are safe, my friend!"

"And you too," replied Cornelius contemptuously.

"Don't think ill of me for my apparent abandonment of you," said Armand: "I had most particular reasons."

"It appears so," answered our hero, moving quickly on.

"Why do you go so fast!" asked the other, "has any thing happened? are you hurt?"

"No."

"Where are are going then?"

"Home."

"No where else?"

"No."

"Shall I accompany you, my friend?"

"No, no."

"Good-night then—good-night! this is my path. Take care of yourself!"

"I need not return the advice, Armand,"

replied Cornelius with a sarcastic smile, that curved his lip like a rippling wave on the face of the ocean, which silently speaks the agitation beneath.

On arriving at the barracks he found Bryan waiting for him at the entrance with a letter in his hand, which he snatched hastily, supposing it, in his uncalculating fixedness of thought on the one great purpose of his mind, to be in some measure connected with his approaching meeting. He tore it open, and started back with conflicting emotions, when he read it to be an invitation for that evening to a party given by the Duchess de Polignac, and at which it was well known to him the queen had promised to appear. His heart throbbed quickly, and seemed almost to rise in his throat. He felt for an instant rooted to the spot. He had longed for this invitation, which had been promised him, and procured for him by his colonel, with a boundless impatience. It was the first time he had obtained the actual honor of being admitted into the private society of the queen. It was known that nobody was invited to parties where she went without the name being submitted to her, and he had here the proof that she had sanctioned and approved of his approaching her presence for the first time, at the very moment that he could not, dared not avail himself of the opportunity. For an instant he resolved to go—to catch one glimpse of her at all hazards—to hear her voice once more—be presented to her, and then fly to justify her name, or perish in the proud distinction of being known to her on a footing of honorable acquaintance.

But his delicate sense of propriety forced him to abandon this intention as soon as it was performed; for he thought it would have an air of gasconade, thus to throw himself into her presence, on the point of an affair which the next morning must make public, be its results what they might. He therefore stepped quickly to his room, desiring Bryan to go and seek Father O'Collogan on the instant.

"Faith, and you'll find his reverence first yourself, Master Cornalius—as it's my place to walk up stairs after your honour," said Bryan.

"Why where is he?"

"Where would he be but in your honour's room, waiting for you, wid a letter from the ould master?"

"Good God! from my father!" exclaimed Cornelius; "I had never thought of him! how is my nature changed, to forget him at such a moment! what sufferings may not be this hour preparing for him should I fall in this meeting! —But no matter, it must be."

Father O'Collogan sat waiting for his young friend, anxiously wishing for his coming, that he might hear the contents of the letter. When Cornelius entered, the priest put it before him on the table, with a significant look of anxiety and pleasure.

"Not now, my good Sir," said Cornelius with emotion, "not to-night, I cannot venture to read it now."

"Why what's the matter with you, child?" said the priest, in surprise: "why it's from your Father, agrah!"

"Even so, Sir—I cannot indeed till the morning—or perhaps late to-night, but not now, I am going out on most urgent business."

"Business, arrah then what business, may I be bould to ask, Honey?"

"Why the fact is, Sir, that it is somewhat which concerns her Majesty—so you see that I cannot."—

"See that you *can't!* oh, by the powers I see it clear enough that you *can* though, do whatever you plase. I knew well there was something in the wind when I saw the Duchess's sarvant coming with that billet with the big seal on it; why then long life and success to you my darling I say; then the queen has sent for you at last! I knew what it would come to—your fortune's made!"

Cornelius, shocked at the mischief he had done by thus committing the name of the queen to the incautious keeping of the priest's imagination, saw that he had but one course to pursue in order to save all risks of mis-statement. That was to tell him the exact truth of his situation: he did so therefore briefly, explaining in as few words as possible the cause and circumstances of the quarrel.

"So you see, my dear good Sir," said Cornelius, finishing his recital; "you see it will be quite useless to interfere or dissuade me—honor and duty command it—I must fight this man."

"Why then, thunder and 'ounds, to be sure you must!" exclaimed the priest; "who the devil thought of dissuading you to the contrary? is it me? far be it from me to stand before a christian soldier and his duty!—my darling boy, I wasn't twenty long years chaplain in the Irish brigade for nothing. By my sowl an you must fight him sure enough, and kill him too, plase the Lord;—and what's his name, my honey?"

"That I never enquired, Sir, but here's his card."

The priest took it, and holding it up to

the fading light close to the window, read it twice or thrice over, and then exclaimed in a voice approaching to terror—

"By the powers it's too true—it's the Black Captain himself! Captain Alexandre Le Noir of the Chasseurs! I would not wish to frighten you, my darling boy, but in troth I fear you hav'n't long to live!" "Why so, Sir?" said Cornelius smiling; "do you know this formidable fellow?"

"Faith I do, to my cost, agrah; for he took the life of two of my best friends in the brigade, besides breaking Captain O'Mahoney's thigh with a pistol bullet, and running Sub-Lieutenant Woolohan through the lungs under the ramparts of Strasbourg."

"Then, my good father, I take their cause as well as my own on this sword," said Cornelius, as he buckled on his belt, and gave directions to Bryan to take his pistols out of the clothes-press where they were deposited in their case.

"Oh the devil's the fear of you, if courage

could do it, I know very well," said the Priest; "but he's a terrible fellow that Black Captain, as we used to call him in the brigade. He always snuffs his candle with a bullet, and he calls the waiter at his hotel by the report of a pistol."

"Well, Sir," said Cornelius, "if I fall by his arm, it is in a good cause at all events."

"Aye," replied the priest, "and it won't be for want of masses any how, if your sowl stays long in purgatory—lave that to me, my darling."

"Now God bless you, my dear Sir!" added Cornelius solemnly, after he had completed his arrangements, and dispatched Bryan with a note to one of his comrades, requiring his immediate attendance to accompany him to the place of meeting. "God bless you, Sir, and if we part for the last time, I trust to your friendship to break this matter to my father—to tell him I thought of him at the last—and to explain that if I did not read his letter—it was only that I feared—"

"Why then what's the use of bothering me with all this now?" said the priest. "Hav'n't you time enough to open your mind while we're going to the ground?"

"To the ground, Sir! why you don't mean to come with me, surely?"

"*Don't* I indeed? you've a very odd notion of my character, Honey, if you think I'd let a friend be in the way of going out of this world, and not see him safe, and give him a blessing at the end of his journey. No, no, that's not the way in the brigade, let me tell you. Come along, come along, my jewel."

Cornelius's friend was quickly with him; and the party, entering the Park through the *Orangerie*, arrived soon under the palace walls, and they saw by the lights streaming from the windows of the apartments occupied by the Duchess de Polignac, a group of ladies standing in the recess of a window, looking out, and apparently admiring the varied effects produced by the expiring daylight, and the young moonbeams sporting through the branches of the copsewood which skirted the lake called *La pièce Suisse.* Cornelius looking up, suddenly distinguished, or fancied, or hoped that he saw the Queen. A pang shot through his heart, he felt it sinking, and putting his hand upon his breast the locket of hair met his touch. He stopped for a moment, and unperceived by his companions drew it forth, imprinted on it an impassioned kiss, threw his eyes a moment towards the window, and felt his bosom glow with zeal and courage as he marched forward.

Under the wall of the Menagerie, which stands outside the park and close to the road leading to St. Cyr, they saw the figures of three men, who stood in consultation as Cornelius and his friends advanced. The tall form of the Black Captain was not to be mistaken. The parties soon took their ground, and their pistols were put into their hands. No one perhaps ever fought a premeditated duel without becoming pale as he stood before his opponent. It is a nervous moment for most men, an awful one for all. Neither Cornelius nor his enemy were exceptions to this rule, but the rush of blood to their hearts was no proof of fear. They stood sternly looking at each other for a moment, and Father O'Collogan declared that they might have been mistaken for a couple of the statues in the park, while the cold moonbeam streamed across their pale profiles and motionless forms.

"The Lord steady your arm, my boy!" exclaimed the priest in a fervent but faltering tone, as he walked out of the line of fire, with the seconds and Bryan, whose teeth chattered together as he attempted to mutter an "Amen!"

"Where will you hit him, Le Noir?" asked the Black Captain's second, as he moved aside.

"In the head," replied he.

"Oh, the murthering thief!" exclaimed the priest, wringing his hands. "The black villain!" cried Bryan.

The signal given, both pistols went off at the same instant. The captain remained steady on his legs. Cornelius tottered a step or two, and his hat fell.

"He's a dead man, heaven receive his sowl!" cried the priest. He rushed forward with Bryan and the seconds, as Cornelius stooped down to the earth, and when they reached him he had picked up his hat, and replaced it on his head.

"The shadow of your cockade saved you, Sir," said the black captain coolly; and it might have been so, for the ball passed just above it through the hat, grazing Cornelius's hair.

"Draw your sword, Sir, and defend yourself!" continued the determined duellist; and before either Father O'Collogan or Bryan had time for an exclamation, the combatants' weapons were crossed and clashing.

"Stop, stop!" cried the Black Captain's second, "my friend is bleeding."

"'Tis nothing," said Le Noir fiercely, and shaking his left hand to motion off his friend, a stream of blood issued from it, for, as it had hung loosely by his side, Cornelius's ball had shattered two of the fingers.

"If you are much hurt, Sir," said Cornelius, dropping his sword's point,—but before he could finish the sentence his antagonist called out

"Come on, come on, Sir, no babbling!"

Cornelius raised his arm once more. He knew that his life depended on his instant exertion, and that he had no chance of escape in a scientific contest. He therefore sprang forward with one bound; and receiving the point of his opponent's sword slightly in his left arm, he made a thrust, and felt the hilt of his own weapon strike hard against the buttons of the coat, as the blade went through the heart and body of his foe. As he attempted to pull it out, the huge carcase fell against him, and as it dropped heavily to the ground, a convulsive heave of the chest, and a deep groan, left it a breathless corpse.

The friends of the unfortunate victim were astounded. They could not for awhile believe the result that was before their eyes; nor imagine the possibility of his skilful arm having been baffled by an untried boy. Cornelius lingered horror-struck on the spot, and gazed upon the livid countenance with great agitation.

Father O'Collogan in vain tried to awaken a spark of life by his pious ejaculations. Bryan trembled so violently as to require the help of his master's second to lead him from the ground; and the whole party reached the barracks in bewildering doubts of the reality of the awful scene.

CHAPTER VII.

The reputation of this affair with the Black Captain became a moral passport for our hero's admission into all the best society of Versailles. When Cornelius wiped his enemy's blood from his sword, he seemed at the same time to relieve his heart from the load which, in the first moments after their contest, had lain there so heavily. He had a clear conscience, his nerves were strong; and he had all his life learned lessons of fortitude and the praise of military feeling. He had been accustomed to tales of warfare by his father, had seen a duel or two in his boyhood, and had frequently witnessed the bloody contests of rival factions at the fairs and patterns in his native country. Above all he glories in the cause in which he had risked his own life, and in which he had taken that of another; and if at times some feeling of regret did arise at his having shed the blood of a fellow-creature, he reflected that it was but perhaps the opening act of a deep drama; for the stormy aspect of things told him he might frequently require a bold heart and a sharp sword. Distinctions of all kinds flowed in upon him. The peaceable members of society felt grateful to him for having ridden the world of a pest, and even the quarrelsome were rejoiced at the disposal of the bravo who occupied the first station on the fighting list. Cornelius's immediate comrades in the guard felt his exploit as their own, and were proud of the doer, as partaking in some way of his celebrity. He was presented to many persons of rank, was assured of immediate promotion, and seemed fairly to have made his first step towards a prosperous career. Father O'Collogan was greatly elated by the glory of his young friend; and Bryan Mulcahie held his shoulders full as high as he had carried his head before, while that seemed in his estimation of its loftiness to touch the very stars. In proportion as our hero was raised, Armand, as he merited, sunk in the world's esteem. Deeply humiliated, he almost entirely disappeared from Versailles, and was frequently seen lounging among the popular meetings of Paris, with a gloomy and discontented air.

Cornelius took all his honours with modesty and moderation; but now fairly admitted as one in the most intimate circle of the queen's friends, and occupying the station which he felt his own, in virtue of his zeal, if not of his services, he had reached the summit of his desires. To see her, to gaze, as he frequently did, for hours together, on her beauty, to hear her, to listen to her animated conversation freely poured out before him—sometimes even to be addressed by her, and to be permitted to reply—what more could he desire! The rest at least depended on himself;—to think of her by day, to dream of her by night, to wear her lock of hair upon his heart, and to vow his whole life to her service. The particular state of our hero's feelings at this period was developed in some fragments of prose and verse, the former too unconnected, and the latter too imperfect for publication. The prose was merely the rambling utterance of conflicting feelings; the poetry, passionate addresses to his idol, but written in moods of too much sincerity and real emotion, to allow of the artificial graces of composition. The documents served, however, as records from which to draw many conclusions, that the more scanty detail of facts would scarcely have warranted.

The disunions among the States General every day presented the most formidable aspect. The National Assembly commenced its self-created career; the power of the King was defied, and he himself set at naught. The Bastile was taken. Tyranny was chased from the land, having previously been rendered so vapoury and impalpable, that like the body of a magician, it left no shadow on its path. But the fifteenth of July, the day after the fall of the Bastile, when the power of the crown was virtually crushed beneath its ruins, the king appeared in the midst of the National Assembly, addressed them in the sincerity of his moderation, was heard with applause, conducted by the people to his palace, and once more possessed the semblance of his state. He deceived himself then, as he did at every step of his gradual disgrace, into the belief that his good faith would beget sincerity in the assembly, and that having acknowledged their rights, all might yet go well. The queen felt differently, and her daring and insulted spirit frowned at the storm whose violence it could not quell. On the day following this memorable visit of humiliation, Marie Antoinette implored the king, as the only hope against the evils which pressed down their authority, to instantly convoke the Notables of Paris, and give them the powers which the Assembly had wrenched from the States General and made its own.

But Louis rejected her proposal. Instead of taking that bold step, he repaired to Paris the next morning, and by displaying himself, humiliated as he was, to the people, he set the seal upon their sovereignty and his own subjection.

From this period no chance of good existed for the queen, and she appears to have almost abandoned all hope of averting the fate she saw preparing. Her arguments to arouse the king to a sense of his danger or his dignity fell blunted against the silken sloth by which his spirit was encompassed. Without a hold upon the nation, or a party in the state, she had but one duty to perform—to follow the fortunes of her husband, and to soften by her sympathy the fall which her firmness could not prevent. During the remaining months of this eventful summer she passed much of her time at the Little Trianon, that favourite retreat, where the elegance of her taste had had such ample field for developement, in transforming the mathematical insipidity of French gardening into the romantic varieties of an English park. If any doubt could exist as to the unfitness of Marie Antoinette for an intimate connection with the nation she ruled over, the Little Trianon is still the evidence of it. That heart must be a hard one, of him who can roam through this enchanting desert at the present day, pace the curved walks, linger on the borders of the lakes, muse on the rustic bridges, or stroll through the lovely village, without feeling a throb of anguish as the mind turns to her who created and adorned the spot. And in recalling her innocent enjoyment of this place, and marvelling that it should stand isolated and uncopied in the country, we can fancy an analogy in its neglect and her persecution. Both the queen and her pleasure grounds were in a taste too accordant with nature to suit a people so artificial. The remark of La Bruyere, that the French wished their masters to be serious and severe, may be fairly illustrated by the taste of their gardens; and their feeling for their king is like that for their flower plots—

that they may be raised up or trampled down at pleasure.

Cornelius had full liberty to enter the Trianons, even when the queen and her party were there. Of this he had never availed himself; for great as was his desire to throw himself continually into her presence, his sense of propriety was too acute to admit of an intrusion on her private pleasures. One evening, however, he returned home early from Paris, where, as was his constant custom, he had been passing the day, less from curiosity to gaze on buildings and promenades, which had but little attractions for him then, than from his desire to watch the progress of the public spirit, and by learning accurately the state of feeling against the queen, to be perhaps enabled, in ever so trifling a degree, to counteract its effects. He was fatigued and agitated; for in the simple habit of a citizen he had mingled with the throng in the Palais Royal, and listened to the abusive tirade of a vulgar demagogue against her whom he believed to be the very essence of all that was pure and good. The absolute necessity of restraining his indignation threw all its violence inwards; and when he reached Versailles, his suppressed rage seemed to call for some soothing remedy. His steps naturally turned towards the Trianon, then occupied by the king, the queen, and a few chosen friends, from those of the courtiers whom they esteemed the most.

As he was known to the porters at the gate, and possessed the countersign for admittance, he had no difficulty in entering the grounds, but that which arose from his own timidity. He paused as he put his foot within the precincts which he was wont to consider sacred; and he asked himself if it was delicate or just to use his privilege for violating the privacy before him. His doubts were, however, put to flight by a distant view of a female group within, and he could not resist the desire of observing the pursuits of this rural party, and judging between the fact of the recreations of the Trianon, and the calumnious accounts which were received by the public. He passed therefore to the left, and wound through the path that leads behind the circular pavilion appropriated to the queen's music parties. As he moved on he heard the tones of a harpsichord accompanying a female voice; but it was not that of her whose tones or whose presence could alone have power to soothe him then. He walked forward, and looking to the right down through the willows and drooping acacias whose branches floated on the lake, he saw a boat rowed by two men in peasants' dresses, but whom he soon recognized to be the Count d'Artois, the king's brother, and the Duke de Luxembourg. Three ladies sat in the boat, and amused themselves by throwing crumbs of bread to the swans, who pursued them at full sail, with curved necks and anxious beaks, raising a froth round their feathered prows, as they cut through the rippling track formed by the boat before them. The disguise of their rustic costume could not deceive Cornelius as to the forms of the ladies, and he knew one to be the queen, the other her favourite friend the Duchess de Polignac, and the third the Princess Elizabeth. As he followed with his eye the course of the boat, he marked a party standing on the opposite bank of the lake ready to receive it. He took his station at the foot of the little round tower called *La Tour de Malbrouck*, as the boat was moored close to the steps of the Miller's Cottage, and he saw the queen handed on shore by the king, in the dress of the *Bailly* of the village, which part he filled in that day's rural pageant; and the whole party moved along towards the house appropriated for the residence of the rustic magistrate. The various cottages were occupied by their noble tenants, who put on for the occasion the habiliments suited to their harmless masquerade. One was the simple *curé*, another the miller, a third a farmer, and so on; and every one assumed, for the time, as much of the manners of the characters they personated, as was consistent with the talents of the several actors.

As Cornelius gazed on this extraordinary scene, and saw the semblance of contentment which reigned around him, he could not help moralizing for awhile. He mused on this mockery of happiness, and would have fathomed, if he could, the depths of pride, profligacy and ambition, which he believed to be hidden under so many humble habits. He thought he could discern the courtier's treachery but ill concealed by the homely air which sat uneasily upon him; and in the gait and gestures of the village dancers, he fancied he could trace a mixture of vanity and falsehood. But when, as he followed the movements of the different parties, he came once more in view of that which surrounded the king and queen, and saw her looking on with the composed expression of real pleasure, and him with an air of calm enjoyment, at the occupation of an attendant who was milking the

Bailly's cows, Cornelius thought that he had at last found a pair, one of whom was formed permanently to fill the character he personated for a day, and the other to enjoy the real delights of a life, the temporary representation of which was planned from her heartfelt taste for its reality. "*There* are no faces," exclaimed he half aloud, "to tell the hypocrisy of the heart; but a sincerity that sanctifies the whole. Heavens! what a pity that yonder king cannot sink at once into the obscure enjoyments of the lowly class he represents this moment, and that she, so fitted to adorn and elevate the humble pleasures of life, must be doomed to an existence of burnished state, that bows down her happiness, as the brilliant sun-beam withers the flower it shines on!"

The impression left on our hero, by the scene which he witnessed, was of a nature too melancholy to be really soothing. He quitted the place by an outlet different from the way he had entered; and he thus saw for the first and last time the idol mistress of his heart and soul, in the character which suited her the best. This was the latest of those pleasure parties in which Marie Antoinette was permitted to shake off, even in seeming, the formal cares of royalty. Many of those who formed her society on these occasions were soon after dispersed abroad; among them, the Count D'Artois and the Duchess de Polignac: and he who wanders now in the well kept, but dreary gardens of the Trianon, marking the tenantless cottages, the lonely groves, and empty temples, may let his fancy shadow forth the graceful form of the queen, surrounded by an imagined group of joyous friends,—and thus people the scene, which would look less desolate than now, if the wild weeds and tangled shrubs were suffered to shut out the memory of its former aspect.

As Cornelius walked slowly along, outside the deep ditch which fences the garden towards the west, he heard from within occasional bursts of laughter, as if the thoughtless courtiers had no heed for the dangers which seemed hovering over the land. Two voices in deep conversation in the walk which runs close to the edge of the ditch, formed a contrast to these unmeaning sounds. Cornelius was no listener, but having caught the first words, the voice which uttered them contained a spell which attracted him towards it in his own despite.

It was the queen who spoke; and there was in her tone a deep seriousness, as if her heart was in the words she uttered.

"Alas!" said she, "what can I do to please them? is not my life devoted to my husband, to my children, and to them; but—no, they will not allow me to be their friend."

"They are growing quite infuriated against you—these pleasure parties are marked with particular obloquy," replied the voice of a man, whom Cornelius could not recognize.

"And would *you* have me abandon these only resources now left me?" said the queen in an affecting tone.

"You *must*," answered the voice.

"I will not," exclaimed she with an expression of pride, and something of resentment. No, I will not, at the command of an norant and ungrateful rabble, be driven from e only consolation left me for their baseness. tell you, in the words of Madame de Maintenon, I am on the stage, and must submit to be ssed or applauded."

"Recollect," said the voice, "that our great ncestor Louis XIV. danced on his own theatre, ut gave up the pleasure when a poet wrote rses to prove its impropriety."

"You are always apt in reply," said the ueen; "and I should be deeply influenced y your advice on all matters, were you not tinged with the odious principles that are road, so fatal to the country, to the king, nd to us all."

"A great revolution is at hand—the king ould become its chief," replied the voice with mness; and our hero, recollecting that these words were a few months before uttered by the king's second brother, the Count de Provence,* had no hesitation in believing that he was the Mentor of his sister-in-law at this moment. He looked through the spaces in the shrubbery, where the figures passed, but he could only distinguish glimpses of the rustic robes worn by the queen, and the cassock of him who personated the curé. A few words more, pronounced in an under tone, were inaudible for him, but just as the speakers turned into another walk, he heard Marie Antoinette say with great emotion,

"Well, since it must be so, I give up the most innocent enjoyment of my life, in obedience to the cruel voice of the people; but it will be of no use. Every concession will but hasten the crisis!" and here the conversation died away.

Cornelius reflected on the speech he had that day heard from the ruffian orator of the Palais Royal, and on the applauding shouts of the

* Afterwards Louis XVIII.

listeners. He repeated the last prophetic words of the queen, and unconsciously exclaimed aloud—

"Then let us be prepared!"

"Prepared!" echoed some one close behind him; "prepared for what, my friend?"

Our hero turned shortly round. He was unarmed, but fearless. He recognized the speaker, and distinguished his voice at the same moment. It was Armand who stood close by him, wrapped in a cloak.

"Prepared for what, Cornelius?" reiterated he.

"For the courage of our enemies, and the cowardice of our friends," returned Cornelius, with a determined and reproachful air.

"Come, come," cried Armand, "forgive me that affair, my good fellow. I bear you no malice, believe me, although your conduct has blasted my reputation perhaps for ever. You *must* forgive my conduct."

"Forgive it!"

"Aye, and forget it. Men must submit to circumstances; and I am no more than other men. Consider how I am situated—how much hatred I excite from the mere chances of my fortune—matters quite out of my control. I am surrounded by dangers, and must meet them by temporizing with events. Adopted by the queen, I adore her. Doubt me not, Cornelius—at this moment you see me lingering round the spot she inhabits, in hopes of catching the sound of her voice, for I dare not look upon her face: but what can I do? my very attachment to her is a crime in the eyes of the people."

"The rabble, you mean," interrupted our hero; "the rabble, who, though they may possess the seeds, cannot from the very nature of their pursuits, have time for the cultivation of refined sentiments, or comprehend the gratitude you owe the queen. Is that the ordeal you would be judged by?"

"They are all-powerful—or will be so soon, my friend."

"Brute ignorance can have no power that I ill own," said Cornelius.

"I must though," answered Armand, "remember I myself am of the people, and must el their cause my own."

"What," cried Cornelius, "is this then your eed? I know what these words would say. The cause of the people!—abused and misapfied phrase! But your views are changed, it eems. The people!—do you then abandon your oyal patroness, to whom you owe every thing? Do you give up all your high aspirings, and esolve to sink yourself into the mob?"

"No, I adore *her*—I repeat it; but I confess I do feel a stir in my plebeian blood, when I hear the people calling for their rights. In fact I have made my choice. I will not stand in the ranks to which my brother may be opposed. I am a citizen, and will act as becomes my station."

This tirade made just its proper impression on Cornelius, by shewing him that his quondam friend, who lately held his nose so high, as if he would not smell the very name of the people, had now changed sides, because the people's heads were towering above his own. Cornelius continued the conversation till a late hour that night, and he found that the ci-devant Marquis de Rencontre was, indeed, reduced to the rank of simple citizen, by the operation of personal fear, a powerful instrument in such times for making converts to any cause which seems to flourish. Armand was evidently deep in the secrets of the Parisian proceedings. His long absences were now accounted for. He talked freely with our hero, whom he evidently esteemed and confided in—but not enough to commit himself. He spoke only as a patriot, not as a conspirator: but, amidst all his reasonings, he protested an affection and attachment to the queen, which seemed to break out every moment unpremeditatedly, like a beam of light on the gloomy tenor of his discourse. Cornelius was determined not to lose sight of him, for he saw how valuable he might prove as a means of counteracting the machinations of which the queen was intended to be the first victim. They parted, therefore, with a promise on the part of Armand to see Cornelius often, and to keep him informed of the state of the public mind towards the queen, as far as his opportunities might allow of his understanding its movements.

For two months more, the elements of the revolutionary tempest were preparing themselves in the depths of the Parisian mind, and bubbling fiercely up to the surface of society. The Assembly, which was supposed to represent the nation, was merely a mirror which reflected the semblance of public feeling. It repeated the frantic gestures, and shewed the distorted features of the people; but it gave no insight into the tumultuous passions which throbbed in the pulses of their hearts. In fact, the nation was not represented—and its Assembly was a mockery; for it stood forth itself in all the power of individual existence, and it outvoiced the clamourings of those who called themselves its organs. The people proclaimed themselves omnipotent; and rightly. It is not the assertion of their sovereignty, but its abuse, which makes them hideous in the eyes of thinking men.

Versailles, during the time immediately preceding the catastrophe which shattered its prosperity, was a scene of continual agitation and alarm. Many of the cold and calculating nobles had begun to withdraw from the field of the forthcoming contest, and left it to the occupation of those whose desertion might have given some chance for safety to the country. Private councils, which could effect nothing to restrain the headlong march of events,—and public cabals, by which it was hastened—ill conceived plans for prevention of ill, and impracticable projects for its cure—such were the combinations of confusion and incapacity, which stood opposed to the rushing torrent of the revolution.

The Garde-du-Corps was at this period almost the only sure reliance on which the safety of the

Royal family rested. The whole body of the troops were more or less infected with the spirit of revolt; and it was only those who came in intimate contact with the residence of the court, in whom the least trust could be reposed. The Regiment of Flanders was then stationed at Versailles; and for the purpose of keeping up its good disposition towards the king, and to draw it more closely to his cause, the Garde-du-Corps invited the officers to a repast, for which very splendid preparations were made.

The Garde-du-Corps at this epoch consisted of eight hundred horsemen, a powerful body in common times—but very unimportant then. This force was chiefly composed of young men of the first connections, and their attachment to the king was proportioned to the favour and consequence which they enjoyed. The suppression, in 1775, of *La Maison Militaire*, the military household of the king, threw a considerable share of distinction upon the *Garde*, who thus possessed the exclusive privilege of protecting the Royal person.

But the chief hold on their allegiance, and the best security for its continuance, existed perhaps in the character of their beautiful queen, and the powerful incitements which her service held forth for the chivalrous fidelity of these brave and ardent youths. Her marked distinction of this corps was very early displayed, for during the rejoicings at the birth of the dauphin both she and the king accepted their invitation to a splendid ball, which Marie Antoinette herself condescended to open, by a minuet danced with a simple guardsman, a youth of gay and gallant bearing then, and who may be seen to-day occasionally strolling on the Boulevards—happy in his old age, and in the recollection of that proudest moment of his life.

The repast to the Regiment of Flanders was given on the 1st of September, 1789, and was the chief cause which hurried on the remaining political deeds of that eventful year. The large theatre in the palace was the place selected for the entertainment, and the preparations shewed that it was no common purpose which was meant by that memorable feast. The tables were laid all down the stage, and across the pit, which was level with it, and the benches of which were removed for the occasion. A numerous orchestra was placed in the gallery, and the boxes were filled with the ladies of the court and their friends, all full dressed. The whole extent of the stage was disembarrassed of its machinery, and the large looking glasses, placed in every interval of the side scenes, reflected back the company, the lights, and the decorations. The guests, consisting of the officers of the regiment of Flanders and a part of the national guard of Versailles, were distributed amongst their invitors; and the unanimity of sentiment which prevailed was in harmony with the magnificence of the whole scene. As the feast went on, and the glasses sparkled, the spirits of the hosts mounted with their wine, and the guests caught the flame of that enthusiasm, the train of which was laid so skilfully. The English custom of giving toasts, just then gaining ground in France, was on this occasion successfully adapted to the rising loyalty of the meeting; and when the King's health was given, the band struck up the celebrated loyal and national air *O Richard! O mon Roi!* This was the signal, or at least the impulse, for the grand movement of the evening; for amidst the echoing shouts of "Live the King and Queen!" a deputation of the Garde-du-Corps was dispatched to the Royal apartments, with an humble request that their Majesties would honour the meeting by their presence, and witness the unanimous expressions of loyalty and zeal. It is difficult to say, although many exist to whom the fact must be known, whether or not this was a preconcerted manœuvre, or whether the king was aware of it and prepared to act accordingly. Much has been written on the occasion, for and against this supposition; but every probability of the case seems to imply that the queen at all events participated in the design. It was consistent with the undaunted firmness of her character, and was a brave and spirit-stirring effort to uphold her sinking cause.

When the king, the queen, and the dauphin entered the theatre, by the front door leading under the centre boxes, and opening full upon the assembled company, the effect was electrical; the wildest expressions of enthusiasm burst from all sides; the band repeated the inspiring air: the feasters rose, and glass in hand shouted it in tones of startling fervour; the ladies in the boxes waved their white handkerchiefs, and joined their timid voices to the hoarse sounds below; and the whole formed a chorus of discord more grateful than the most melodious harmony. Amongst the most enraptured but the least boisterous was our hero. The deep emotions of his soul could not in *her* presence find vent, for his respect restrained the outward symbols of delight. He was, however, one of those who followed closest on the royal train, as it returned to the apartments of the king; and when he me back to this scene of festivity he gave loose to his joy. The party at length broke up, and scattering into the court-yards and the parks, their enthusiasm was soon caught by those without, as well as felt by all within the Palace. The soldiers of the Regiment of Flanders were as highly excited as their officers; one of them climbed up the outside of the architecture of the palace to an alarming height, till he reached the windows of the king's bed-room, and shouted *Vive le Roi!* Cornelius was one of those who helped him to descend; and as he reached the ground the report of a musquet told the fate of another of the regiment, who in a paroxysm of loyalty shot himself on the *Place d'Armes*, in mad regret at having listened to some who strove to turn him from his allegiance!

With such results as these before them, the royal family and their party may well be excused if they recovered their confidence in some measure, and deceived themselves awhile. They imagined this occurrence to be the touch-stone of feeling, not only among the military but the people at large; they misconceived (as we generally do events and objects which are near to us) the dimensions of the experiment which had been tried; and they flattered themselves into the belief that the scene just acted in the Royal Theatre of Versailles would be repeated in every town throughout the kingdom. This delusion produced the usual effects on the victims. They talked much, but did little; raised their voices, not their arms; overrated their means and under-valued their enemies; retarded their measures of safety, and hurried on their ruin.

The active agents of the popular party held a different course from this. They saw that there still was danger to their cause; and they resolved that the flame which had burst forth from the embers of loyalty should be extinguished in the blood of those who raised it. The queen and the Gardo-du-Corps were doomed to immediate destruction; and events rolled on.

The interval between the day of the repast

and the fifth of October was not marked by any material occurrence in which our hero was personally concerned. He, in the fulness of his youthful hope, was no doubt deceived like the rest, and could not imagine the possibility of mortal ill to that being whom he elevated above the range of mortality. He almost wholly neglected every thing but his military duties and his devotion to the queen. He fulfilled the first and cherished the latter with equal zeal. His correspondence with his father followed the course of other less interesting affairs: his letters became hurried, unfrequent and rambling, and he betrayed the wanderings of a mind which evidently went astray when it swerved a moment from its one great object. Father O'Collogan saw what was passing with a watchful and gloomy eye: amidst all the simplicity of his nature he possessed a great share of the shrewdness which is common to his countrymen, and his dark anticipations burst forth in many a conversation, exclamation, and quotation, which we shall not stop to record. Bryan Mulcahie viewed the aspect of affairs in a very different light from his confessor. He had become gradually reconciled to his situation, had made himself master of a few important phrases of the language, and being a cheerful and obliging fellow, he had ingratiated himself into the good graces of two or three of the men servants and five or six of the females of the neighbourhood. He had been at Paris more than once; and observing the idleness which was predominant, the neglect of business, the continual talking, singing, dancing and fraternal embracing in the streets, he pronounced the French to be "the pleasantest people in the whole 'varsal world out and out;" and the catastrophe which was at hand burst upon him like a thunder-bolt.

But Bryan Mulcahie did not stand alone; for such was the ignorance of the cabinet of Versailles as to what was coming to pass, or the absurd affectation of indifference towards it, that on the morning of the fifth of October, the day which was virtually the last of the royal power, Louis, its hapless representative, went out on a shooting party to the woods of Meudon! Courier after courier arrived from Paris, report followed report, and alarm succeeded to alarm; but it was not till the Parisian army had actually begun its march for Versailles, that a messenger was dispatched to summon the king to his palace; and as the monarch and his train wound their way through the woods which skirt the road by Meudon and Sevres, they could hear the shouts and shots, and mark the tumultuous advance of the infuriate horde, which poured along the line of road parallel to their path.

At the time of the king's arrival at the palace the day was far gone, and Marie Antoinette, filled no doubt with presages of the coming evil—but such forebodings as strengthen, instead of unnerving a mind like hers—had taken her way, without friends and with but two menial attendants, to her favourite gardens of the little Trianon, in whose beautiful walks and bowers she then lingered for the last time. Cornelius was at the palace. The guard had been doubled in consequence of the alarming rumours from Paris, and he was one of those on duty. But if even he had not been so, he would have stationed himself somewhere near the person of his idol—for he knew her to be in danger. He had that morning received two hurried billets from the capital, in the hand-writing of Armand, one by the post, which had been written the previous night, telling him to be on his guard, as a crisis was near. The next was still more brief, but more explicit. It was dispatched in the morning by a private messenger, and contained but one line:—

"Look to the queen—you shall see me to-night."

In consequence of these ominous words, our hero set off for the palace, where he was met by the adjutant, who warned him for the augmentation of the guard. He was ready for the call and was, with several of his comrades, standing in the hall of the Garde-du-Corps in the palace, observing the king's arrival, and anxiously looking for that of the queen, when Count de St. Priest, one of the ministers, came from an adjoining chamber with a note in his hand, in hurried agitation, and said :—

" Gentlemen, which of you can take this to her majesty, at the Trianon? There is no time for forms—will you, Sir?" addressing our hero, who stood next to him.

Cornelius took the note, and with a bounding heart, and winged steps, he soon reached the entrance of the Trianon gardens. He burst past the porter, merely uttering "for the queen;" and he was abruptly proceeding in the direction to which the porter pointed, when he was stopped suddenly by the sight of her he sought, as she sat on a bench not many paces from him. She was dressed in a plain white gown, and her head was covered by a large straw hat, the leaf of which concealed her face and her profusion of hair. She held a handkerchief in her hand, and as Cornelius silently marked her, forgetful wholly of his mission, he observed her to put her handkerchief more than once towards her eyes. She raised her head, and looked towards the west. Thick clouds were gathering, and as she cast her brimming eyes upwards, she wrapped a shawl close round her, warned by the rough blast which shook off the yellow leaves from the trees, and whirled them through the air. She then rose and advanced a few steps towards the Temple of Venus, just opposite, and close to which is still the bench where she sat that evening; and she was apparently going to enter, when she observed Cornelius. His hat was in one hand, and he advanced holding the minister's note in the other. He attempted to utter the name of Monsieur de St. Priest, but the words faltered on his lips. She observed his agitation, and took the proffered paper. While she ran her eyes over it, her two valets, who had till now respectfully stood far from her, approached rather nearer, and when she had finished, she calmly turned round, and motioned them to follow. Our hero drew back to let them pass. She walked forwards, and addressed him as he followed.

"And the king, Sir? has he returned?"

"I saw his majesty safely enter the palace," replied Cornelius.

"Thank God!" uttered she: "and my children,—the Dauphin and Madame?" recovering herself, and giving them their titles, as if the first natural expression was less dignified than it ought to be.

"Let your majesty be tranquillized," exclaimed Cornelius: "they are safe in their apartments;" and then he added in a tone of sudden animation; "fear nothing, I beseech your majesty, for aught that is yours! No danger can approach, though it may threaten you."

She stopped for a moment, and turned her eyes upon his glowing countenance, and then said with much emotion—

"Ah, Sir!"—after which she made a long pause, as if shaking away the doubts that overcast her mind—but she added in a quick manner, and with her smile of unrivalled sweetness,

"I know the zeal of all your corps, and believe me, Sir, I have not forgotten, nor am I ungrateful for your individual proofs of attachment. Your reward is I hope at hand."

"Reward!" exclaimed our hero—and he would have added that he was more than repaid—or words of deeper energy—but he felt his voice fail him again; and she perceiving the strength of his emotion, and probably seeing deeper into its source than even he did, moved forward at a quickening pace, and prevented the utterance of his high-wrought feelings.

They went quickly on by a private way, which had been planned by the queen, and executed under her eye, but which does not now exist—a passage from the palace to the Trianons, winding round by the lower gate in the Rue Maurepas. This was a trellised walk, thickly planted at each side with rose trees, jessamines, and odorous shrubs, which crept up emboweringly, and formed a delightful shade in summer time. At the then advanced period of the season the roof and sides had lost their leafy covering, and were sufficiently open to admit a full view of whoever passed along. The wall of the park was close at one side, and as the queen moved forward with a quick but steady pace, not looking to the right or left, our hero who had recovered himself, and respectfully followed some yards behind, observed a small piece of rolled-up paper flung from outside the walls, and dropping through the trellised work on the path between him and the queen. He picked it up, and unfolding it he read, in the ill concealed and evidently agitated hand-writing of Armand,

"Beware of this night. Your life will be attempted. Your natural courage must be your guide, but your only safety is in flight. A friend is watching you, though you believe him false—but gratitude to a queen is not incompatible with duty to our country. Do not be deceived—the hour is come!"

No sooner had Cornelius read this, than he saw it was meant for the queen; and while he advanced to present it to her, Armand from behind the wall pronounced his name, and added "I will meet you at the Dragon's gate."

Our hero presented the paper to the queen, and told her how it had reached him. She took it and read it without any visible emotion. She then tore it, and as she flung the scraps away, exclaimed,

"If they come to murder me, I will die then at the king's feet—but I will never fly!"

"For the love of heaven and earth let me entreat your majesty to pause a moment," cried Cornelius with much agitation. "I know the writer of this paper—let me seek him; his intelligence may be important."

"I know him, too, Sir," answered she indignantly; "ingrate that he is, he is unworthy of my fears or your enquiries. Let us on to the palace."

They were here met by some of the ministers and the great officers of the household, who came to escort the queen; and Cornelius slipped away, and went for a moment to the gate named by Armand, determined to hear what he might choose to communicate.

His former companion was waiting for him just outside, in a recess formed by one of a new range of houses about that time commenced, but the completion of which the events of that evening put a stop to. Breathless, pale and agitated, Armand beckoned Cornelius towards him, and threw fearful looks around, dreading the chance of being detected in contact with any one belonging to her service to whom he owed every thing.

"Well, Armand," cried Cornelius, "be quick —I have but a moment."

"And I not so much, Cornelius," replied he. "Come here, close to me;—this is a dreadful honor—I have done my best to save her—I saw you across the wall giving her my note—Heaven grant she will follow my advice and fly—Her life is lost—trust to no appearance of calm, the plot is laid." He was here interrupted by loud vociferations which proceeded from the frantic rabble, headed by the Poissardes, in the open callousness of female depravity, as they came up from all the avenues in the direction of the palace.

"Is that all?" cried Cornelius impatiently. "Have you nothing to communicate but impotent advice, and these too tardy warnings? I must leave you—my duty lies within these gates."

"Which I dare not enter!" said Armand. "My fate is cruel—bitter—maddening! Here, Cornelius, here, you love, you adore the queen, and are fitting her service. I alas! am not. I feel my weakness, and blush and tremble while I confess it. but I must go through with—must fulfil my destiny.—Do you mark this portrait?"

While he spoke and hurriedly disengaged the queen's miniature from around his neck, Cornelius gazed on it and listened to him with fixed impatience.

"This is that portrait which she fastened round this neck with her own gracious, beauteous hands," continued Armand. "I durst not keep it—and I have striven but cannot force myself to destroy it—If found on me, it would cause my instant death."

"Oh give it, give it to me!" cried our hero; "how poor a price would death be for the pride of its possession!"

"It is yours—I meant it for you, and now I give it to you," said Armand hurriedly; and as he pressed Cornelius's hands, in which the miniature was firmly clasped, he burst into convulsive sobs. Cornelius was touched with his evident sufferings, and softened by the proof he had given of his sensibility towards the queen, and his kind feelings to himself, "Come, Armand, come!" said he, "this is the moment of your redemption. Come in with me —the gates are closing—come back to your duty—your honour—your home—come in, come in!"

The porters within were now on the point of closing the gates, alarmed at the increasing crowd which poured down from the Avenue de St. Cloud. They called to Cornelius, whose uniform made him an object for their interest —and they told him to hasten or they must be forced to shut him out to the fury of the Parisian mob. He caught Armand's arm for the purpose of leading him in, but the loud bursting shouts of the terrible Poissardes struck again on the hearing of the terrified and trembling apostate.

"Oh no, no, 'tis too late. Oaths of horror bind me—and those sounds are the heralds of death to all within these gates—Oh God! which way must I turn.—They come, they come—let me fly—if seen with you I am inevitably ruined —away, away!—but tell the queen, oh, tell her!"—Another hell-burst from the approaching furies sounded still more close. Armand fled, in the direction of the sound—and as Cornelius entered the gate, the last tones of the renegade's voice, which mingled with the grating of the bolts and hinges, were shouts of "Live the people! Live the nation! Down with the tyrants! Down with the king! Down with"—but our hero hurried away, lest he might hear a more damning proof of the coward's shame. He held his hand firm on the picture, against which his heart throbbed strongly, and he soon mingled in the ranks of his fellow guardsmen within the palace walls.

CHAPTER IX.

THE tumult without the palace was answered by the consternation within. The turbulent energy of the mob had its counterpart in the perturbed incapacity of the courtiers. The first marched straight and firmly to their object,—the latter wavered on every step down which they were descending to destruction. Thirty thousand men, intermixed with bands of those female fiends before-mentioned, poured into Versailles that day This collection has been called, by a stretch of historical courtesy, the Parisian army. La Fayette was nominally its chief, but he was set in motion by its spontaneous movement, and once on march with the rest, he found it as impossible to command them,

the leader of an ill-tuned orchestra, whose
e tones are overpowered by the jarring dis-
ds around him. To oppose the hostile opera-
ns of this resolute multitude, the Regiment of
nders, the National Guard, and the Garde-
Corps, were arrayed in the Place d'Armes.
ffectual as their opposition might perhaps
e proved, they were not, however, allowed to
ke any. Incertitude as to the steps to be
en, prevented any attempt at vigour. As the
t clamours were heard, it was decided that
royal family should immediately retreat
ler the escort of the garrison, to Rambouillet,
re to concert on some measures of safety.
t some fatal and treacherous cries of *Vive le*
i! induced the ministers to abandon that plan.
e odious Poissardes, with their large white
ons, which they declared destined for purposes
ards the queen too horrible to mention here,
r forced their way into the court yard of the
ace, and insisted on seeing the king. He
sented to their admission, heard their clamor-

ous demands for bread, and apparently succeeded in quieting them; for they retired, shouting his name, and singing in a frantic chorus, the song which was so celebrated at the birth of the dauphin, and which ran thus :—

CHANSON DES POISSARDES.

Ne craignez pas, cher papa,
D 'voir augmenter vot' famille,
Le bon Dieu z'y pourvoira:
Fait's-en tant qu' Versailles en fourmille;
'Y 'eut-il cen Bourbons cheu nous
'Ya du pain et du laurier pour tous.

THE POISSARDES' SONG.

Have no fear, father dear,
To see your brats encrease about you,
God is good, to send them cheer;
Let Versailles swarm with them; nor doubt you,
That though a hundred Bourbons call,
We've loaves and laurels for them all.

During this scene, several of the members of the assembly crowded round the queen, and one of them put an anonymous letter into her hands, which had just reached him, and which announced her intended assassination the next morning. She read it calmly, returned it to him from whom she received it, ordered the group to retire, and coolly said, "to-morrow will prove to you how necessary repose is to-night."

Matters appearing thus calm, the Garde-du-Corps were ordered to break up from the Place d'Armes in front of the palace, and to retire to their barracks. This movement was considered by the impetuous mob as setting the seal upon their triumph, and their violence consequently knew no bounds. They assailed the Garde-du-Corps with vollies of stones as they retired, and they fired several musquet shots, by one of which one of the guardsmen fell mortally wounded. The troop did not return these assaults, but on arriving at the barrack found that it had been pillaged by the rabble, who had then scattered all over the town in straggling parties, obtaining such refreshment as they could; but committing no other outrage than the one just recorded. Upon the ministers in the palace hearing these events, a second resolution of a retreat to Rambouillet was decided on. The royal carriages were ordered, and the family preparing for the movement, when, just as the horses were about to be harnessed to the carriages, and the crowd looking on, dissatisfied but passively, a young man, who was the servant to General Beauharnois, the husband of Josephine, afterwards Empress of France, seized one of the bridles and called aloud to the assembled multitude for assistance, to prevent the escape of the king, and the destruction of the people's liberties. By this prompt and daring act this groom decided the fate of his sovereign, and was the source of his mistress's after-elevation. An actor of the theatre of Versailles stepped forward to his help—the rest of the mob followed his example—the traces were cut—the horses turned into the stables—and the monarchy overthrown. The news of this measure spread dismay within the palace.

But one course was left, for that night at least, and the king followed it, by throwing himself under the protection of La Fayette, and his army, and professing a confidence in them; which was honest on the part of the king, most just as it regarded the general, but madness as applied to the armed rabble. The main body of the Garde-du-Corps, who were boiling with rage, and from whom some dangerous outbursting was expected, were ordered off to Rambouillet, and the king was thus left with no attached defenders, but the handful of the *Garde* actually on duty in the palace; for the whole of the Regiment of Flanders had gone over to the Parisian army, and joined in all their movements.

It was thus that matters stood when the royal family yielded to the persuasions of La Fayette, and retired for the night. This excellent, but incompetent man, believing all safe and right, went himself to bed, and the king and most of those within the palace followed the example.

The courtiers and their followers dropped off one by one to their several rooms; the long corridors and galleries were gradually deserted; and scarcely a light was seen to glimmer in the vast extent of the palace, except the flitting taper of some domestic, winding up the stairs to his attic room, or pausing for a moment at some window, looking on the court yard, in hopes to catch a glimpse of what was passing in the gloom without. The queen, worn out and overpowered, flung herself into bed at two o'clock in the morning, and ordered her two attendant ladies to do the same. But their attachment to her told them that their first duty was, in this instance, disobedience. They quitted their royal mistress's apartment; and oppressed by a presentiment of danger, they took their post in the anti-chamber, close against the door of the queen's room; and thus slumbered away in the stillness of the night, which was for some hours unbroken, but by the whispers of the Garde-du-

Corps, who kept watch in the great room outside the antichamber, and by the tramp of the centinels who paced the court-yard and gardens.

Contrasted with the desolate grandeur of this scene in the House of Royalty, was the ruffian sublimity which reigned without. The evening and night were wet, windy, and dark. The ragged clouds swept rapidly through the heavens, scattering showers from their broken skirts, as each irregular gust dissolved their fragments into rain. The ground was wet, and the large unsheltered *Place d'Armes*, with the wide avenues and streets, were covered with the outstretched bodies of thousands of wretches, who grouped themselves at random in their gloomy bivouac. As many as were provident enough to get shelter had filled the houses, and occupied the beds, to the exclusion of the trembling inhabitants who kept watch in their parlours and kitchens; and these intruders consisted of all those who had any pretensions to decency in station or feeling. The rest, a large majority, were the refuse of the Paris Faubourgs, beings so contaminated as to glory in their own vileness, and to feel a pride in the brutal degradations which they volunteered. Reeling with wine, and reckless of danger, they flung themselves down on the readiest dunghill, and the overflowing gutters washed the carcases whose impurity was congenial to their streams. Discontented mutterings and low curses mingled with the whistling blast that at times bent the flexible stems of the trees, and shook the rain drops on the slumbering groups below. Their irregular weapons clashed confusedly together, blown down from their ill-arranged piles by the wind; and an occasional scream from a cracked trumpet, or the roll of an ill-braced drum, roused up some of the fierce horde—who sunk down again, growling curses on the disturbers of their desperate repose. Females too, the very outcasts of the vile, were abundantly scattered over this peopled desolation. They were to be seen huddled together in dreary fellowship, fatigue and sleep lording it over their depravity,—and drooping their heads upon the breasts in which their woman's milk had turned to gall. Children were there—the urchin followers of the throng, weeping in cold, and wet, and hunger; some calling for the parents they had straggled from, and others slumbering in the arms of wretches, who cherished their offspring from the brute instinct with which the tigress suckles her whelps.

Such were the beings who waited no incitement but the dawn, to plunge into deeds of frenzied atrocity.

At half-past four o'clock the drowsy eye of morning opened from its cloudy lids upon the scene. The restless mob, irritated by the night's discomforts, their bodies unrefreshed, their hunger unappeased, their vengeance unglutted, rose from their heaps, and shook their draggled garments in the face of the dawn. The inhabitants of the palace mostly slept; a few of the more nervous had passed the night in snatched and wearying slumbers, and started at every blast of wind that moaned through the doors or window-shutters. None but the resolute band of Garde-du-Corps, among which was our hero, had thoroughly outwatched the night; and they, as they perceived the streaks of morning light stealing through the scanty foliage of the woods, prepared themselves to meet a day that bore a kingdom's fate upon its wings.

A few straggling shots fired from the Place d'Armes was the only signal for the attack on the palace. In the next instant the court-yard was filled, and the great doors forced open by a simultaneous burst. The chief rush of the mob was up the grand marble staircase which led to the queen's apartments, and at the head of which opens from the landing-place the hall of the Garde-du-Corps. Next to this room, which was occupied by the guard, was the antichamber, where the queen's ladies had stationed themselves with their women. At the first alarm several of the guards rushed out to the head of the stairs, and a fierce conflict began. Many of the assailants fell, and their furious companions trampling across the bodies, completed the death which the bullets of the guard had commenced. The imperfect light gave the advantage to the defending party. They made great slaughter, and but two of their brave troop were killed. The wounded were dragged back into the hall, and the whole body at length retreated thither, and barricadoed the door inside. But this delicate barrier of gilded and painted pannels soon flew shattering in, before the force of plebeian blows; and the guardsman who stood in the gap, was partly protected from the hacking sabres of the assailants by a defence formed by his carbine, which, after having discharged, he placed across the door, and held firmly with each hand. The fragments of the wood broke the deadliest of the blows, and he only received two cuts on the head and face, which covered him with blood, but did not move him from his post. His comrades behind him discharged their pistols under his arms, and thus for several hour-like minutes, kept the whole crowd at bay. The intrepid sentinel looked frequently round, and cast his straining glances at the door of the queen's antichamber, as if only thinking of her! At length in the midst of this tumult, the terrified women could not resist their agitated curiosity; and one of them opened the door to see what was passing. At the instant she put forward her pale face, the bleeding sentinel, Cornelius—for it was he—cried in a hoarse voice, "Save, save the queen! fly and bolt the doors on us!" The spectral face disappeared; and as the door closed and was bolted beyond, our hero, exhausted and again wounded, sunk on the floor, and gave free passage to the rushing horde.

In the close wedged crowd but little injury was inflicted on the remaining guardsmen. The mob hustled in so thickly that they impeded their own wish for blood, and in the confusion and delay of forcing open the door of the anti-room, the queen had time to spring from her bed, awakened by the screaming women. She fled, undressed as she was, towards the little private door leading to the king's apartments; her first distracted thoughts turning towards him and her children. With feelings of horror, she discovered that this door was fastened outside, and all the efforts of the women to force it open, with their shrieks for help, were almost drowned by the uproar of the mob from the rooms beyond. In the midst of their despair, one of the king's valets hurrying though the passage behind, opened the door; and the whole party, headed by the queen, rushed towards the king's bed-room, where the children were found, the king himself having gone to seek their mother. He soon returned, and the scene of momentary happiness, in the midst of the misery around, must be imagined better than it can be told.

While Cornelius lay bleeding and faint upon the ground, his only care was to preserve the miniature of the queen from the trampling feet of the crowd, which struck upon him and his wounded comrades. With his hands covering the treasure which lay on his breast, and his face turned towards the wall, close to which he lay, he heard a low muttering voice pronounce his name. He looked faintly up through the standing mass, and by the light of the torches which had been carried in, he discovered the pale face of Armand, who was groping round, and evidently searching for him on the floor. The strong impulse of self-preservation made him answer the call, and Armand soon relieved him from the pressure. He stooped down, and tearing off Cornelius's coat, unperceived by the mob, who were then rushing through the forced entrance into the antichamber, he wrapped him in the short cloak which had hung on his own shoulders. He then drew him towards the landing-place, and was preparing to convey him down the stairs, proclaiming to those who advanced, that it was a wounded patriot whom he was saving; when a tall and powerful man, half dressed, in black breeches and stockings, and his shirt-collar flying open, burst his way through every impediment, advanced towards our hero, looked at his face a moment, lifted him up as though he had been a child, and carried him down the stairs upon his shoulder, without speaking a word, and, followed by the astonished Armand, who, it must be told, had taken no part in the attack, but had waited tremblingly below, till, all resistance being over, he was enabled to seek his friend without danger to himself.

Cornelius, revived by the air, soon recognized the face of his preserver, as his own lay close to it, over the broad shoulder which bore him. It was Father O'Collogan, who, on the first alarm, had rushed to the scene of action, in turbulent anxiety for his young friend,—having prudently divested himself of his cassock, his band, and hat—symbols of his profession, which, if displayed to the mob, would have doomed him to destruction, but without which he readily passed through the heterogeneous crowd, as an able-bodied light-clad patriot. Arrived at the foot of the stairs, calling out for room, and suiting the action to the word, by shouldering right and left through the living mass, he was met in the entrance-hall by Bryan Mulcahie, who having passed a sleepless night in the deserted barrack-room, haunted by fear of the Black Captain's ghost, and anxiety for his master's safety, had sallied out at the early report of fire-arms, furnished with a bludgeon, and, hurrying towards the palace with the crowd, had entered it in the hopes of finding Cornelius, alive or dead. It was a happy thing for both Cornelius and his supporter, that Bryan could not make himself intelligible to the crowd; for his mingled lamentations and abuse of the people, as soon as he saw his master bleeding on the priest's back, would have betrayed all, and proved a sentence of death to the whole party. Father O'Collogan pushed Bryan aside with the rest, as the poor fellow came blubbering up to his wounded master; and he was fain to follow, without farther explanation, the long strides of the priest, who neither stopped nor spoke till he deposited his burthen in one of the wards of the town hospital, where Voisin, the chief surgeon, was already busily employed in dressing some of the wounded mob. Armand kept close to the body of his former friend; and while he and the priest satisfied themselves, by the assurances of the surgeon, that his hurts were by no means dangerous, Bryan, seeing nothing short of death in Cornelius's livid face and motionless body, began deliberately to chaunt forth the Irish howl.

"Wirashtrew! Wirashtrew! Oh, why did you die! Why did you lave your father and your people, Wirashtrew!"

"Howld your tongue, you stupid divil!" cried Father O'Collogan; "how dare you have the impudence to tell your master that he's dead!"

"Wirashtrew! Wirashtrew!" exclaimed Bryan, wringing his hands.

"Whist your noise, then, I tell you again, you spalpeen, or I'll lay the print of your cheek on my four fingers and thumb!" vociferated the priest, foaming with rage.

"Arrah, why did you die!" continued Bryan, looking woefully on Cornelius; when the secular arm of his indignant confessor was raised high against him, and the iron fist came sledge-like upon his ear, and laid him sprawling on the floor. At this instant five or six of the wounded guardsmen were brought in by some of their companions, who had made their way through the rabble; but scarcely were they received into the hospital, when a group of the ruthless wretches pursued them, and attempted to force their way through the outer room, to put them to death.

The priest's presence of mind was here conspicuous, and of the utmost importance. He advanced to the outer room with great calmness, having first snatched up some of the instruments of surgery which lay on the table; and his shirt being covered with Cornelius's blood, he had altogether a very professional air. Thus accoutred, he presented himself to the furious mob, and met their murderous threats by a profuse display of all the wine intended for the use of the sick, and by assurances that there were none of the Garde-du-Corps in that part of the hospital. M. Voisin, the surgeon, had in the meantime ordered the attendant *sœurs de charité* to hastily clothe the wounded guardsmen in the coarse covering used for the poor patients; and this being promptly done during the priest's parley with the ruffians without, no trace was left by which they might distinguish their foes from their friends. The only person in danger of falling a victim was Bryan; for when the good women saw him lying crying upon the floor, they supposed him to be wounded with the others, and they accordingly proceeded to cover him up with the long brown linen wrapper. He kicked and struggled with his usual violence, and exclaimed against this proceeding, until the clash of the weapons, and the hideous vociferations without, brought him to reason, by nearly depriving him of his senses, and he passively submitted to be lifted up by four or five of his kind-hearted attendants, who placed him, more dead than alive, in the same bed with a livid-looking guardsman, whose ghastly countenance close by poor Bryan's cheek made him fancy himself already laid in his grave. Armand had voluntarily thrown himself into another ward, and lay with a throbbing heart, and the bed-clothes covering his face, when the rabble burst in, accompanying Father O'Collogan; and seeing nothing to indicate the military character of those they observed, they were persuaded that the guardsmen had been carried off by some private passage to another part of the building; and thus baffled in their first bloody intention, they dispersed towards the palace, in hopes of finding some readier victims for the sacrifice they intended.

While this was passing at the hospital, the palace presented a scene of indescribable terror and confusion; the splendid halls and tapestried apartments being the theatre of bloody and protracted outrage. As soon as the queen fled from her sleeping-room, and the doors of the anti-chamber were forced open, some of the Garde-du-Corps had dexterously thrown themselves between the mob and the room where they supposed she was still in her bed. They there renewed the contest with the assailants, who were at last persuaded by the assurances of the household servants that the queen had escaped. Quitting the point of immediate attack, they then rushed by another passage towards the gallery called *l'œil de Boeuf*, hoping there to intercept her flight; but she was safely sheltered in the apartment of the king, where with her children in her arms and her husband beside her, she was firmly prepared to meet whatever might happen. The small but devoted band of the Garde-du-Corps, on being assured of the queen having left her bed-room, passed through it into the *œil de Boeuf*, and by barricadoing the doors, were able for awhile to resist the efforts of the grenadiers of the Parisian National Guard to burst them open.

But as the resistance must have been in the end unavailing, one of the guardsmen, named De Chevanne, resolved to devote himself a victim to the chance of saving his comrades; and he threw himself into the antichamber alone—in the midst of his foes. Struck by this act of isolated intrepidity, the assailants paused, and he in a few moments of earnest eloquence made one of those effective appeals to the turbulent passions of men, which are oftener successful in France than in all other countries of the globe. In a few minutes the National Guard and the Garde-du-Corps were seen like brothers exchanging cockades and caps, embracing and shouting together, "*Vive le Roi! Vive la Nation! Vivent les Gardes-du-Corps!*"

From this moment all was safe. The impulsion spread like wildfire through the troops, and from them was caught by the people. The palace was cleared, and instead of the atrocious threats and murderous vociferations, mixed with the clash of arms and tramp of a furious multitude, the profaned but now uncrowded corridors and halls echoed the joyous embracings of the household, the boisterous gratulation of men, and the hysteric laugh of women, all nearly as frantic with delight as they had so lately been with fear.

For some hours after this, a boisterous incertitude prevailed throughout. The straggling elements of the mob power, which had been decomposed during the night, were now rapidly massing once more, under the effect of the stimulus which the attack on the palace had given to all. The *Place d'Armes*, the court yards, and the terraces were thickly thronged with the armed multitude, who insisted with imperative demands that the king and his family should abandon Versailles, and accompany them to Paris. Resistance was at this crisis vain, and it is useless to record the names of those who advised an impotent refusal. The king gave his consent to the measure. "I confide myself to the people," said he, "let them do with me as they please;"

and the preparations for departure were hurried on. But the outrageous impatience of the rabble would not be satisfied without the visible testimony of obedience to their commands, and the actual presence of their victims. They vociferated in angry tones for the queen's appearance at the balcony which opens from the room where Louis XIV. expired, upon the marble-paved court called *la Cour de Marbre.* Imprecations and threats accompanied the call, and those who surrounded the queen and who heard the tone, tremblingly intreated her not to appear, as they little doubted their intention to fire at her as she stood, and thus complete their diabolical design against her life. She alone stood calm and courageous at this awful moment. She took her children one in each hand, and stepped out upon the balcony with a confident mien. "No children; no children! send them back—stand out alone!" shouted by a thousand voices, were the horrid orders which assailed her. She did not tate a moment, but putting the children in at the window-door behind her, she turned round again towards the crowd, and raising her eyes and her clasped hands to heaven, she stood awhile in the undismayed conviction that each successive moment was her last. A murmur of astonished approbation rolled hoarsely through the throng, and of all the sinewy arms that bore a weapon among it, but one was raised to take her life, thus offered as it were to their assault. One ruffian, flushed with fury and covered with clotted blood from the morning's conflict, stood at the corner on the left of the *Cour de Marbre*, on the very spot where the assassin Damiens had placed himself to strike at the heart of Louis XV. Seeing the queen thus exposed, within thirty paces of his design, and while the rushing tide of popular inconstancy was on the point of turning in her favour, he levelled a musquet at her breast, and snapped the trigger. The piece went off; but the bullet flew high in the air, almost perpendicularly over the roof of the palace; for an arm beside the murderer had struck the weapon up at the very instant of its being discharged. The wretch looked round on him who had frustrated his aim, but did not recognise Cornelius in the pale and wounded being who leaned against the corner of the wall beside him. Our hero, who, devoured by agitation, had insisted on crawling from the hospital, weak as he was, and had placed himself in this position, supported by Father O'Caltogan, thus saved the life of her, for whose service he lived, and instantly knew in the would-be murderer, that very soldier of the Regiment of Flanders, who a short month before had in an exposure of unprincipled loyalty climbed up the palace walls to shout blessings on the king! Prompt as the voice of the storm, which answers the lightning's flash, the voice of Cornelius followed the flash of this inebriate madman's weapon. "Long live the queen!" once more burst from his pained lips, and the words were repeated in a shout from the tumultuous assemblage which rung from the fifty niches in the surrounding walls, filled with the busts and statues of emperors and kings.

The queen retired with unruffled and dignified demeanour, and then the loud voice of the sovereign people called for the subject king. As he came forth, a new exclamation arose. "To Paris! To Paris!" was the general cry, and the monarch with meek loyalty replied, "Yes, my children, since you wish me to accompany you to Paris, I consent to go—but on the one condition, that I shall not be separated from my wife and children." Cries of *Vive le Roi!* were the reply, and when he next asked security for his faithful guards, "*Vivent les Gardes-du-Corps!*" answered his demand. The names of the king and the nation were then blended in a general shout, and a stunning discharge of artillery and musquetry from the throng rattled the window frames of the houses, and shook the hearts of the inhabitants of Versailles.

At one o'clock, under a beautiful sky, and

warm sun, the procession moved forward on its five hours march towards the capital, with circumstances which do not come within the range of this story; and Marie Antoinette threw back her farewell looks on the splendid residence of fifteen years, the scene of pleasures and grandeurs, and admiration, and influence, that rarely fall to the lot of the most fortunate of queens.

Cornelius lingered till the last moment; nor would he consent to the entreaties of Father O'Collogan for his return to the hospital, until the echoes of the royal carriage were inaudible, and his dimmed and swimming eyes scarcely saw the confusion of the procession, as it slowly moved along the broad and crowded avenue, which leads in a direct line from the Palace-yard towards Paris.

Armand had early stolen away, no one knew whither: having satisfied himself of Cornelius's safety, and thus eased his conscience, in some measure, from the bitter reproaches which were ever rising up, self-created, in his mind; for he felt that in preserving this devoted adherent to the queen, he did more for her than could be effected by any actual effort of his own dastard fidelity. Bryan with difficulty submitted to the orders of his master, to remain in the hospital; but when he saw him return leaning on the arm of the Priest, he applied himself with assiduity to every office which his wounded and afflicted master required at his hands.

CHAPTER X.

THE public events which followed close upon these memorable transactions are in the memory of every one; and having no immediate connection with our hero, need not be snatched from history to swell the limits of a story like this. A mock enquiry into the outrages perpetrated against the Royal Family was made by the National Assembly, and ended as might be expected, in nothing being done to punish the guilty, whose impunity was high above the reach of their accusers. Some questions were put to Marie Antoinette, as to her personal knowledge of what had passed. "I saw all—I felt all—and I have forgotten all,"—was her reply.

Two observations on these events—fatal alike

to despotism and true freedom, seem obvious—one with relation to the king, the other to the country. Louis should at that pregnant moment, the fifth of October, have taken one of two decisive courses. He should have fought or *abdicated*. He should have boldly placed himself at the head of his army—or wholly prostrated himself at the feet of his people. It was clear that blood must flow in the struggle. The only question was, whether it was to be that of the king or the crowd. *His* weakness was to have steered a middle course at such a crisis—*theirs* to have upheld his means of continuing it after. They should have at once *deposed* him. For, having sunk him in the depths of contempt, it was vain to keep up his shew of power; and the principle of overthrowing the monarchy by years of disgrace, was at once unworthy of the nation, and cruel to the individual. As for the queen, her days of wretchedness had commenced—to end but with her life. She took possession of the Tuileries, her palace-prison, with an aching mind; and for many dreary months endured those preparatory trials, for sufferings to which neither history nor fancy have recorded or imagined a parallel.

Cornelius submitted with an impatience which may be well conceived, to a fortnight's confinement in the hospital of Versailles. His imprudence in going out on the morning of his wounds, and mixing in all the agitations of the day, added considerably to the injury he had received. Anxiety for the queen cut deeper than the sabres of the mob. During this imprisonment, Bryan never quitted his master for an hour, but Father O'Collogan went almost daily to Paris to learn intelligence of what was going on; and though Cornelius's sanguine mind saw matter of high hope in the apparent loyalty which was loudly professed by the capital, the Priest, in the bluntness of his sincerity, took especial care that his young friend's recovery should not be hastened by any delusive expectations, which his gloomy forebodings might have power to chill.

He saw things in the very worst possible light, and it was in the nature of his diction to clothe his dark thoughts in still darker words.

"Every thing's lost entirely, out and out, my jewel," said he one day on his return from Paris, as he threw himself panting into a chair by the side of Cornelius's bed.

"How, what? explain yourself, my good Sir—has any thing happened to the queen?" cried Cornelius, starting up.

"Keep yourself cool—keep yourself cool, honey," replied the Priest, "nothing has happened to her *yet*. She's in her snug quarters, 'till they take her off by pison or otherwise—and his majesty nor the childern isn't murthered—at least they wern't when I left Paaris—so make yourself aisy about them."

"What then, Sir, is it? explain yourself for heaven's sake."

"What is it! why, it's every thing that's bad, that's what it is. It's the clargy—it's religion—it's the Catholick Church they're attacking.—

But it stands on a rock, and the divil himself couldn't pull it down! That's what they're at. They're threat'ning to rob the church, and to scatter the clergy all over the wide world;—that thieving assembly! I tould you all along what it would come to."

"Why, what is done?" asked Cornelius.

"Every thing, I tell you; they are going to cut down the benefices, and to rob the cathedrals, and to get rid of the bishops, and to banish the curates,—I see it all straight forment me, although it hasn't come to pass *yet*."

"What has put all this into your head, my dear Sir?"

"I'll tell you that then;—it's no later nor this morning, that I went into that sink of the divil, the *Palais Royale*, and I heard a villain, mounted on a stool, tell the blackguards round about him, every word that I now tell you; and, surely that, when he had finished, he took a book out of his pocket, and what do you think it was? why, the Bible, the Bible!—you know the Bible, Cornelius,—that's the Ould and the New Tistament; you know that?"

"To be sure, Sir."

"Well then, he took the Bible, and he dashed it down in under him, and jumped upon it, and tore it in pieces!"

"And what did the people do, Sir?"

"Why, they danced and sung, and blasphemed, and swore vengeance against all the kings and queens, and priests on the face of the earth, —that's what they did, unfortunate wretches that they are!"

"And what did you do, Sir?"

"What did I do! why I did what they did to be sure; I buttoned my brown coat up about me, and I danced and sung, and shouted my way through the rapscallions, as merry as the best of them:—

Si Romæ fueris, Romano vivito more.

When in Rome, no man
Should act unlike a Roman.

That's my motto on such occasions, and the

Lord forgive me, if I did a sin in saving my life for his sarvice, and for yours, my dear child, for I thought of you all the while, and didn't like the notion of being torn to pieces by the ruffians, (which they surely would have done, if they knew who it was that was in it,) and lave you in this miserable place to die in despair, without a friend to pray one *profundis* for your sowl."

Such was the general tenor of the priest's communications, by which he meant to comfort and support his friend's drooping spirits; and on such foundation as the event just narrated, he built, and after all, not unwisely, his predictions of the sea of troubles which was about to overflow the land.

Cornelius, by the attention of his surgeon, and those exertions of mind which aid the efforts of art, recovered rapidly from the effects of his wounds, and the fever which followed his incautious exposure to agitation and fatigue. As soon as he was allowed to venture abroad, without actually trenching on the outward limits of prudence, he repaired to Paris, there to satisfy himself as to the situation of the queen. Accompanied by Father O'Collogan, he reached the Palace of the Tuileries, and being known to some of the servants, he readily obtained entrance, and an opportunity of seeing one of his acquaintance, a gentleman, who held an office near the person of the king. From him he learned every particular which had occurred since the outrageous events at Versailles, including the dispersion of the Garde-du-Corps, and their being replaced in their attendance on the royal person by what was called the constitutional guard of Paris. Our hero also learned that several of his comrades in the gallant defence of the Palace of Versailles had been recognised and insulted by the mob; and he found that a strict avoidance of publicity became essential to that personal safety, which he only valued as it might afterwards afford him a chance of devoting himself to the well being of her for whom he felt himself every hour more deeply interested. He therefore took measures for removing from Versailles, where he was so generally known, and in a few days he finally abandoned that town, where in the short space of five months, such a rapid rush of incidents had taken place, chequering his heretofore tranquil life, and nurturing emotions and passions, before unknown to him, but now hurrying him on to the completion of the destiny in whose impulsion they had birth.

He took a small lodging in one of the suburbs, half-way up the hill of Montmartre, where he was gratified in the feeling that he could distinguish the residence of the queen, among the mass of surrounding buildings; and whence he almost fancied himself to look down, like some unknown, but protecting spirit, watching over her safety. Bryan Mulcahie was here more than ever useful to him, and he found in the faithful assiduity and the quaint humour of this artless creature, a relief from the oppressive reflections which crowded on his solitude. Much as Father O'Collogan felt desirous of accompanying his friend, he had duties still more urgent to perform. His parish required his care more than ever, for he found all his exertions unavailing to keep the stragglers from his flock from becoming every day more numerous, in spite of all that his energetic efforts could effect, in the way of persuasion or threat—the hopes of heaven, or the promises of hell. His natural buoyancy of mind kept him up under these vexations, and he trudged frequently along, with a staff in his hand, to pay a few hours visit to Cornelius at Montmartre, and unbosom himself, while partaking his homely repast, of his sorrows and prognostics, pastoral and political.

Cornelius passed, in this unvaried retirement, the whole of the latter part of the year 1789; and the frosts of winter began to dissolve under the tepid breath of the succeeding spring, ere he found any adequate excitement to make him quit the hill to which he had thus become, as it were, naturalized. His occupations during the earliest of these dreary months had been all of the mind. He had no bodily employment; and his only exercise was his daily walk into Paris, to acquire intelligence of the queen. He saw her frequently, omitting no opportunity of watching her whenever she went out to drive, and being a regular attendant at the chapel of the palace twice every week. There he used to watch her as she paced the long gallery through ranks of military, who were more her jailers than her guards; and he followed every movement of her soul-lit eye, which pierced the serried files, to discover the friends whose looks gave warrant of their attachment. Among the faithful band she never once missed our hero, whose passion grew and ripened in the beams of her speaking glance. He made some attempts at study, but they were in vain. His fancies and his feelings went on in eddying circles, set in motion by the one passion, which had sunk so deep in his heart; and every power of reflection or imagination revolved in confusion round the point on which his fate seemed fixed.

During this period the queen bore with the fortitude and dignity which were her most striking characteristics, all the griefs that crowded on her. She devoted herself totally to her duties as a mother, and superintended in every thing the education of the unfortunate dauphin and his sister. She refused every solicitation which was pressed upon her to quit France alone, and leave the king and the people to complete the formation of the constitution, without any possible pretext for accusing her of its delay. She replied, to those who advised the measure, that she never would quit the king and her children; that if she thought herself the only mark of public hatred, she would willingly sacrifice her life; but that she saw that the destruction of the monarchy was the object in view, and that in abandoning France, she would only gain the cowardly advantage of saving herself.

She also rejected every proposition to go to the theatre, or have concerts at the palace; but she dined twice a-week in public with the king, according to the ancient custom. To form a real notion of her feelings at this period, we must hear her speak her own sentiments, which were thus expressed in a letter which she wrote to the Duchess de Polignac:—

"I cannot restrain my tears on reading your letters. You talk of my *courage*: it is much less necessary for my own immediate support in these frightful times, than to keep up the spirits of those who surround me. I am oppressed by the heavy weight of my situation; and were it not that my heart is devoted to my husband, my children, and my friends, I should wish to sink under it. But you all sustain me in my trials. I owe it to your attachment to bear up against every thing; but, alas! I bring you nothing but misfortune, and all your sufferings are on my account."

With the exception of going to two or three

parties given by the Princess Lamballe, in her apartments in the palace, the queen remained during the whole of this dreary winter in complete seclusion,—all her conversations with her friends bearing upon the subject of the Revolution, their chief object being to ascertain by what means she had so totally lost the good opinion and attachment of the fickle people.

To recompense her in some measure for the public hostility, and to shew their attachment to the king, the nobility who were then in Paris felt it their duty to attend constantly at the Tuileries, and an appearance of royal power was thus preserved, in weak signs of ceremony, while every essential of authority was rapidly dissolved. A party insignificant less from its numbers than its imprudence, endeavoured to uphold the king's prerogative by an intractable display of loyalty. Women, in their zeal, wore large *bouquets* of lilies, and knots of white ribbons, in contrast to the national cockades, which were almost universally borne by the people. Frequent quarrels took place in the theatres and the streets. The most violent language was held by the royalists, —the sure sign of weakness; and levity and imprudence were throughout opposed to the persevering audacity which struck at the foundations of the throne.

The projects of the republicans advanced so quickly, that many of those who at first opposed the court on just and constitutional principles, were now becoming disgusted, and withdrew from a contest from which they foresaw nothing but mortification and defeat. The royalists, finding this moderate and middle party giving way before the violence of the mob, and perceiving that no barrier existed to keep its overflowings from reaching themselves, were impressed with the necessity of the royal family's flight from a power which it could not oppose. Many plans were therefore in agitation, in the winter of 1790-91, for the king's escape. The most celebrated, the most impracticable, and the most fatal to its author, was that of the Marquis de Favras.

This ardent partizan had formed the project of raising an army of thirty thousand men, to march upon Paris and carry off the royal family. It is most probable that both the king and queen were privy to this design. It is certain that she at least, with the decision which marked her character, had long seen the necessity of the attempt at escape which the king so long opposed, and at length tried but to be ruined by its failure.

The unfortunate Favras, after many efforts to raise funds sufficient for the furtherance of his enterprize, was betrayed by some of those to whom he confided his project, and was offered up a victim to the popular fury. He was hanged in the *Place de Grève*, in the month of February, 1790, and his heroic conduct to the last inspired many others with fresh courage in the cause he died for, while his failure gave a lesson of prudence to those who were pursuing the same object.

Cornelius narrowly escaped being implicated as an accomplice in this affair, and as such, per-

[illegible] [illegible] the [illegible] of [illegible] [illegible] [illegible]. He had heard of the proceeding of [illegible], and in the [illegible] of [illegible] himself in the [illegible] [illegible], he was on the point of joining in the enterprise, and offering his services, when a friend with whom he had [illegible] daily communication, dissuaded him from his intention. No common arguments could have held him back; but the influence of this friend proceeded from a source which we have [illegible] [illegible] [illegible] [illegible]. The name of this person is [illegible] to the readers of the story; but it was that of one well acquainted with the secret sentiments of the queen; and she knew as well the value of her best friends, to either [illegible] [illegible] [illegible] [illegible] [illegible] [illegible] [illegible] example, while she hoped the day to be at hand when they might effectually give their co-operation in some feasible plan of escape. [illegible] therefore, waited anxiously for the [illegible] which were to give due [illegible] [illegible] to the [illegible].

Notwithstanding the [illegible] which [illegible] [illegible] [illegible] [illegible] [illegible] on him, the [illegible] [illegible] over with a rapidity known only to those whose minds are occupied by the never-ceasing contemplation of one adored object. Cornelius's sentiments acquired every day an increasing tinge of that deep devotion which colours the mind of the enthusiast. In proportion as the difficulties of Marie Antoinette increased, so did she appear to his view more admirable, and the changes which seemed each hour reducing her to the level of common life, removed her in his estimation to a distance more elevated for those who really loved her. His views of her character were certainly not dispassionate—for he was incapable of seeing what others thought her errors. But the more strictly impartial the mind that examines her conduct—the more rigid the enquiry instituted into it by the lover of truth, who reads, enquires, and reflects upon her life, the more firm must be the opinion that pronounces her a woman wholly innocent of crime, and whose very failings shine through the thick veil of her miseries, with a light that might rival the virtues of those who are assailed by temptation or wrung down by persecution. The loud voice of calumny, which so long assailed her, is almost mute, because the personal and political hatred which inspired it has nearly died away with the generation to which she belonged. The fact that no one charge was proved against her that would affect her reputation as a virtuous woman and devoted wife, might, even in her life-time, have been thought sufficient to doom her slanderers to infamy—for then the whole pack of human motives were in full chase, from which no character had a chance of escape; and had the faintest shadow of guilt been reflected from an act of hers, there existed thousands of enemies on the watch to embody it into a palpable accusation. But among the volume of slander, and torrents of abuse with which her reputation was assailed, not one *fact*, however slight or isolated, was ever substantiated; while every testimony of those who saw her most, and knew her best, tends to establish her innocence, on every charge

[uch has been written against her, and more
ooken. Loud assertion and whispered inuendo
ive been busy with her fame. Many, no doubt
nposed upon by the hardihood of her calumni-
ors, believed in her guilt upon the assumption
' public opinion—but *now* when all has been
ard against her, which hired traducers could
sert, or credulous dupes believe—now that the
itural weakness which leads men to imagine,
id the vile passions which urge them to invent
of their contemporaries are all hushed, it is
arcely possible that there exists one person
io can believe in her impurity, after having
amined the question of her conduct on the
ot where she lived, and among those of all
rties to whom her life was known.

With such an object in his heart, seen through
e medium of enthusiastic adoration, our hero
andered about the heights of Montmartre, with
sort of visionary elevation of intellect. He has
ood in the early morning, when the winter sun
st peered over the horizon of houses to the

eastward, and listened to the bells awakening the population of the city below, to the labours and tumults of the day; and he gazed with breathless intensity on the sublimity of the vast masses of building stretching far and wide, in which no sign of human life was visible to him, but which covered the arena of conflicting millions, whose struggle shook the world. He has, from another point, watched the red sun sink in dissolving mists beyond the wooded hills of St. Cloud, and throw his burning beams upon the river and the city, making every wave and every pane of glass in which they were reflected, shine with diamond brilliancy. Again he has walked along the ridge, while the night fell thick around him, and the windmills on the summit looked like huge sentinels waving their giant arms. He has looked down where the vapours shut out the view of the city, and listened to its solemn hum, which sounded like the rushing tide; while the lights glimmering through the mists looked like the reflection of the stars in the bosom of ocean, and the steeples of the churches, piercing the vapour, might have been supposed so many tall vessels floating on the surface of the sea. But in all these varieties of aspect, the one feeling mingled; and Cornelius would start in the midst of his abstraction, and rush hurriedly down the hill, nor cease until he found himself in the sight, or at least in the close vicinity, of her whose imagined presence was the inspiration of all his movements.

CHAPTER XI.

It was during the month of March that our hero became suddenly changed in looks and manner. Instead of the indefinite air and vacant expression, which had before marked his appearance, the astonished Bryan now perceived him to move about with a vivacity that he had not for months exhibited, while his animated features seemed worked upon by some great purpose. His ramblings on the hill had almost ceased, and his visits to Paris became much more frequent. Father O'Callegan, who regularly made the journey to Montmartre twice, and sometimes even three times a week, and who had been always sure of finding Cornelius at home on the days appointed, was now often obliged to wait for his return from the city for whole hours beyond his promised time; and once or twice he was forced to go back to Versailles, greatly disquieted at the arrival of written excuses from his young friend, and somewhat mortified by his constant refusal to confess the causes of his protracted absence. Bryan, who talked freely with the priest on this mysterious change, and who was not nice in his conjectures, proposed on one occasion to prove his fidelity by following his master into the town, and watching his movements; but the indignant elevation of Father O'Collogan's clenched fist, and the remembrance of its operations on a former occasion, made Bryan instantly renounce his mean-spirited but warm-hearted intention.

It was some time before the secret of these absences was revealed to the priest, but Bryan was left ignorant of them to the last, satisfying himself with some conjectures as to their cause, congenial to his own natural and national fancies. The fact was, that Cornelius had entered deeply into the plot of several royalists, headed by the Count d'Inisdal, for surprising the guard of the Tuileries, and carrying off the king. This plan was constructed with prudence, was known to both the king and queen, and had every probability of success. Many of the nobles were concerned in it, and the night was at last fixed for its execution. Cornelius quitted his lodgings that evening, leaving every thing in its usual state, so as to excite no suspicion in the old man and his wife who were the owners of the house. He said he was going to the theatre, and he ordered Bryan to attend him, for he was resolved not to abandon him at this crisis, and had stipulated for his being employed as a secret agent in the enterprise. He walked down the hill with a light step, and his only regret was that his solemn oath obliging him not to divulge the secret, he was forced to leave Father O'Callogan ignorant of his departure, and to trust to chance for a safe opportunity of informing him of its results.

The hour of ten sounded from the various

clocks of Paris—the carriages were ready—the confidential partakers in the enterprize at their posts—and the section of the National Guards then on duty at the palace gained over, when the Count d' Inisdal, the resolute chief of the confederates, bent his steps towards the Tuileries, to warn the king of all being in readiness, and to re-assure the spirits of those for whom he and his friends were risking every thing. He arrived at the apartments of one of the ladies highest in the queen's confidence, and having explained himself fully, he begged of her to go down to the queen's apartments, where the royal party were at that moment playing whist, and to get the king's positive consent, that the attempt should be put in execution. An attendant gentleman, also fully in the royal confidence, undertook this office; and entering the chamber, he delivered Count d' Inisdal's message. No one made the least reply. The queen impatient at the king's irresolution, said to him, "Sir, do you hear what has been said?"

"Yes, yes, I hear it," replied the king, continuing his game.

Monsieur, the king's brother, addressing the gentleman with his usual familiar habit, as if he was calling in theatrical language for a repetition of a song, exclaimed,

"Pray give us that pretty verse again if you please, Sir." He then said a word or two to the king, persuading him to reply, but his majesty remained silent; when the queen with her tone of prompt decision, exclaimed,

"It is absolutely necessary, Sir, to say something or other." The king at length said—

"Then tell Monsieur d'Inisdal that I cannot consent to the plan for carrying me off."

The queen, who saw through the irresolution which prompted this dubious answer, hoped by a turn of pronunciation and emphasis to convey an approbation in the very words of refusal.

"You hear, Sir," said she to the gentleman, "you hear the king's reply; and you will not fail to tell it to Monsieur d'Inisdal faithfully.—

The king cannot *consent* that they carry him off."

The gentleman retired; and the queen immediately set about her preparations for flight; not doubting for a moment that the zeal of the party in the plot would make them interpret favourably the words which she had so pointedly uttered. She was busied till midnight packing up her jewels and the few other valuable articles which she meant to take with her; and for several hours after she paced her chamber with anxious steps, looked out at the windows into the stillness of the courts and gardens, and could not persuade herself that the project was abandoned, until the streaks of morning light separated the grey clouds, and dimmed the flame of her solitary lamp.

Cornelius, who had worked up his feelings to that intense pitch suited to an enterprize, in which he felt his whole hopes at stake, waited in silent impatience at the post which was assigned to him. Bryan stood firmly beside his master, not knowing what was coming to pass—but ready to brave any thing, so *backed*. It is unnecessary to dwell on the deep disappointment of our hero, when Count d'Inisdal came to the place of rendezvous about eleven o'clock; and relating to the trusty band assembled for his purpose, what had passed at the palace, and speaking bitterly of the king, he exclaimed—"I understand him —he wishes by this conduct to anticipate consequences, and throw the whole blame on us who devote ourselves for him." A short consultation ensued, and the attempt was totally abandoned.

This failure disheartened the hopes of the royalists. New plans were imagined, but none advanced towards completion. Advice of all kinds was daily offered to the queen, but nothing was effected for her relief. She would in nothing separate herself and her fate from that of the king and her children. Dangers pressed on, but found her undaunted; and one night, when Louis, alarmed for her safety by some random shots fired on the terrace of the Tuileries, flew to her bed room, and found her in the children's apartments, and holding the Dauphin in her arms, he said, somewhat hurriedly—" I have been looking for you—you have agitated me." She replied, shewing him her son, " I was at my post."

As Cornelius's participation in the attempt of Count d'Inisdal was not known to Father O'Collogan, he escaped the reproaches which the worthy Priest would no doubt have poured on him, for not in some way procuring him a share in it—and Bryan, even in his confessions, kept to the last the secret which he had been in a very slight way admitted to, but which he justly considered as no sin of his, whatever might have been its object. Cornelius had for several months received alarming accounts of his father's health, and he had frequent struggles with himself on the question of flying to his parent, or remaining near the queen. Each letter that he received filled him with anxiety, and no sooner had he read it, than he resolved to set off immediately;

but one thought of her—one imagined scene of the dangers which surrounded her—one view of the picture which he wore next his heart, was sufficient to destroy all his filial ardour for the time, and he instantly began to reason with himself on the over anxious view which he took of his father's illness, and to convince himself that it could not be as serious as he feared at first.

But one letter at length arrived, which roused him from this state, and put an end to his self-deceiving sophistries. It was from the Roman Catholic clergyman of the parish in which his father's estate stood, and it gave so alarming an account of this dear parent, that Cornelius was filled with the conviction of the necessity of his presence at home. He gave himself no time for reflection, but wrote hurriedly yet decisively to Father O' Collogan to come to him on the morrow to receive his farewell, and he next proceeded to Paris to entreat, through his friend at the palace, the honor of being admitted to take leave of the queen, having first demanded her permission to absent himself from her service, and stating the urgent nature of the duty that called him away. It happened that just at this juncture two other of the Garde-du-Corps, who had, with him, bled in the defence of the palace of Versailles, were about to quit Paris by the particular orders of the queen, for their lives had been more than once endangered, by their resolute defence of her in public parties, where her reputation had been assailed. They acted from the bold impulse of duty, which told them to court all dangers in justification of her honor. Their attachment was not of that deep and speechless kind, which prompts the possessor to his own preservation on common occasions, as his first duty to her whose service may require the sacrifice of his life on some momentous crisis. Marie Antoinette, anxious to give the most positive token of her gratitude to these her gallant defenders, had appointed this very evening of Cornelius's solicited interview, to receive them in the palace in the presence of the King and Madame Elizabeth. It was an opportune occasion for granting the same honor to our hero; and it was arranged that the three brave comrades should make their appearance together.

At eight o'clock that evening, they were punctual to the time appointed, and entering the palace secretly, and one by one, they met together in the apartment of one of the queen's confidential attendants.* This lady having received them graciously, requested them in the queen's name to accept whatever sum they might severally require to enable them to quit Paris. Cornelius's two companions, took each of them a small sum in gold from the open box, which the lady held in

* Although no name is mentioned in Cornelius's manuscript, it seems probable that this was Madame Campan. In her Memoirs she mentions a circumstance similar to this interview; but it might not have been the same, as she only specifies two Gardes-du-Corps. Though the account of what passed, being almost verbatim the same as here, it is more likely that this was the scene she describes, and that she forgot the exact number of actors in it.

her hands, but he refused respectfully, and with gratitude, stating that a remittance had reached him that very morning, which left him ample means of making his journey. Had it not been so, he too would have freely taken from the stock which was, as it should have been, common to the friends of the hapless owner.

In a few minutes the door of the chamber opened, and the king, the queen, and Madame Elizabeth entered. The three guardsmen bowed with profound respect, and our hero felt his heart throb, and his eyes swim, as had been usual with him on former occasions, of immediate interviews with the queen. She sat down in an arm chair, behind which stood the attendant lady; Madame Elizabeth occupied another close to her; the king walked towards the fire-place, and stood with his back resting against the mantel-piece; the three young men stood facing their royal master; for they owned him still as such, powerless as he had become.

The queen looked repeatedly towards the king,

as if encouraging him to speak, but finding that his timidity would not allow him to break the silence, which was throwing an awkward air of formality over a scene that was meant to be as familiar, as was consistent with her own and her husband's dignity, she spoke as follows:—

"Gentlemen, the king, as well as myself, has wished to see, before your departure, such gallant friends as you have proved yourselves to be to us. We feel, all of us, how much we owe to the courageous attachment, which most probably saved our lives. We trust that this interview may be as gratifying to you, as it is to us. We deeply feel our obligation to you all."

Her voice faltered a little, when one of Cornelius's companions took advantage of the moment to express in a few well chosen words and a collected manner, the devoted fidelity of himself and his friends, and their proud sense of the honor they then enjoyed.

"My brother," said Madame Elizabeth, "wants language to express himself as you deserve, gentlemen, and as he feels,—you perceive his emotion." And, in fact, it was observable; for though he did not speak one word, his eyes were filled with tears, and his lips quivered in his vain attempts at utterance.

The queen was embarrassed at this new proof of the king's tenderness. It was a moment for the bold and manly expression of his thoughts. But his nerves were not able to bear the weight of his feelings; and she spoke again:—

"Now, gentlemen, it is necessary that we retire: nor must you be seen here. You know our situation: we must only patiently bear it, and pray to Heaven for the bright day when we may burst from it. This has been a short interview, but it has proved to you what we feel, as well as could have been done by an age of more ceremonious display. Farewell, gentlemen! Be cautious of your own safety,—we may want your aid again. Farewell."

The guards retired. Cornelius would have given worlds for the power of uttering one word, but his thoughts seemed to die away in their passage from his brain to his lips, and as if their energy dissolved through his whole frame, he trembled with the force of his agitation. The king went out of the room followed by Madame Elizabeth; and as Cornelius closed the door by which he and his companions retired, he heard the queen say to the lady, whom she drew towards a recess,—" I am mortified and sorry that I brought him here—so is Elizabeth, I am sure. —Had he but said to these brave young men but half what he thinks of them, they would be wild with joy;—but he cannot conquer his fatal shyness."

" How little," thought Cornelius, " was the expression of *his* sentiments necessary—for one of us, at least!"

We must pass hurriedly over the leave-taking with Father O'Collogan, as well as the ecstasies of Bryan Mulcahie, at the prospect of once more seeing his " ould mother, the ould castle, and the ould master," and turning his back, as he said, upon "the *desateful*" country, where they cried long life to the king, while they swore they'd be the death of him; and took off their hats and made a low bow to a man, while they put a rope about his neck, and tucked him up to a lamp-iron.

Cornelius's preparations for departure were soon completed. He took but few things of any kind with him,—the rest he left with the priest; and in a state of disorder which he purposely chose, to prove to himself that his absence was to be a short one. He hastened every movement to the very utmost point of despatch. He gave neither himself nor Bryan time for one regular meal. The post-horses were driven at their greatest speed; and the winds and tides were too slow, even when most favorable, for the rapid progress of his wishes. He gave thought no breathing-time; nor did he venture to look back one instant on the scenes he was quitting. His whole efforts were to keep his mind on the stretch, in picturing what was to come; for he feared that if it once reverted to the idolized object he left behind, his high-wrought resolutions would dissolve before the magic touch of memory. In this war with his own inclinations—sleepless—unrefreshed, and every way wretched, he performed his journey by land, and his short sea voyage, and once more touched his native soil, and wound his way along the road which led to his long-loved home.

CHAPTER XII.

CORNELIUS had been absent exactly a year, and the powerful changes which that period had effected in the whole constitution of his mind produced a corresponding appearance in every thing which now met his view. At every step, he saw the same desolate wretchedness, yet nothing was altered which he had been accustomed to witness from his earliest years; but the strong contrast formed by the splendid misery he had been so lately in the midst of, gave an air of tenfold loneliness to the landscape around him. His father's house stood in a wild part of the country, where a heart-broken race of peasantry seemed to have caught their tone from the bleak and cheerless aspect of the scenes they lived in. Rude hills, extensive plains, and dreary bogs, were bounded by the ocean; while the old castle, from which the ancestors of our hero looked defiance on the surrounding tracts, stood forth a solitary illustration of the uncivilized region over which it frowned.

As our hero slowly moved along followed by Bryan, on horses hired at the town where they landed, he suddenly caught the view of his paternal residence; and its old round tower, gloomily contrasting with the modern building in which twenty years of his young life had glided away, brought his mind back at once to those remote associations which a few eventful months had for the time almost effaced. Every scene and every sensation of his early days seemed renewed. Actions and thoughts returned upon him in all the vividness of their first existence, and unlike the mere reflection of memory. He inhabited once more the world of his natural feelings; and his late adventures, and the deep passions which arose from events that looked unreal, now swept before his mind as the phantom pageantry of a vision. Every object which met his view spoke of his boyish days. The mountains, the plains, and the sea, brought home to him the bursts of opening delight which kept pace with his first field sports and ocean excursions. Every tree or rivulet or rock which varied his rugged road, spoke a diction familiar to his fancy, and he appeared to hold converse with a crowd of old imaginings. The dreams of his boyhood came rising into fresh life before him, his energetic grief at his country's degradation, and the wild schemes of redress in which his musings were wont to abound. In the midst of all, the recollection of his father was mingled—in figure, gesture and words—his heart was expanding in the warmth of filial love, and he started and stopped in his reverie, for it seemed to him that his father's form had actually met his eyes. He turned round short, recalled to the observance of his actual situation by this home touch of fancy, and he asked Bryan if he had seen any thing.

Poor Bryan found it difficult to reply to the question, for his mind had been undergoing a process somewhat similar to that of his master; but his feelings, less acted on by visionary flights, and oppressed with some superstitious sentiment of evil, had been silently dissolving in a flood of tears. When he recovered himself sufficiently to speak plainly, he told Cornelius that "he saw nothing but the *model* of his poor ould mother which was continually crossing his path, and he was sure that her *Fetch* if she was living, or her spirit if she was dead, had been every minute at his elbow ever since he mounted the unlucky black baste that his legs were hanging at each side of." This ludicrous avowal of a state of agitation so like his own acted on Cornelius better than all the reasoning in the world could have done; and putting spurs to his horse he went forward briskly, blushing at the self-knowledge of his weakness.

As he approached the precincts of his home, every thing wore a deserted air. It was but little later than noon, yet the cabins were shut up, the ploughs and other implements of labour lay unemployed in the fields, the cattle wandered at random, and no inhabitants were to be seen. Phantasies of all kinds crossed Cornelius's brain. Fears of some calamity pressed upon him, and he unwillingly found that the most superstitious notions were forcing themselves into his mind. He rode on the faster--as if in search of some explanation, but every one appeared to have purposely fled from his path. At length, emerging from a little grove of oak, which skirted the road at each side, close to the foot of the hill on which the old castle stood, he heard a wild cry come faintly down, which carried to his ears the well known death-wail, and seemed to vibrate through his frame.

"Good God! Bryan, did you hear that?" cried he; "'tis my father."

"No, no, Master Cornalius, there's no fear of him—it wasn't him that swept past us just now on that blast of wind. It isn't you that's an orphan this blessed hour, God help me!"

"What do you mean, Bryan?" said Cornelius, glad to catch at even the chance of denial, which the wild superstition of his companion gave to his fears.

"Don't ask me, Master Cornalius, don't ask me—she's gone—I saw her and hard her—and she seemed to touch me as she passed by. Listen, there's the keening again! the Lord rest her sowl!"

And again the wailings were carried towards them by the breeze, louder and more lengthened than before. Cornelius shuddered as he forced onwards at full gallop, yet clung in the midst of his fears to the hope that it was Bryan and not he who was parentless. In a few minutes more he was in sight of the court-yard in front of the house, and he saw it thronged with people of both sexes, the female part *keening*, (as it is called) wringing their hands, tearing their hair, and shewing every symptom of sorrow which is displayed in that part of the country on the death of a friend or protector.

No room for doubt now existed in Cornelius's mind as to the loss of his parent, yet he distractedly asked of the men who crowded round him as he flung himself off his horse, "where is my dear father—is he indeed gone?"

"Oh, Master Cornelius, is it your honor that's in it?" "Oh, the Lord save you, my jewel, is it to-day you're comed back to see this sorrowful sight?" and many such torturing exclamations burst from several lips.

"You distract me," cried our hero; "tell me the truth for heaven's sake, where is my father? Is he, oh tell me, is he dead?"

"Sure enough he's dead, plase your honor, or as good as dead, for Father Keegan is giving him the last sarvice; the Lord be marciful to him, for he was a good master to us!" said one of the weeping men.

Cornelius could listen to no more. He rushed

into the house, and proceeded up stairs to the room where he knew his father always slept. At the door he found a crowd of women, howling in doleful chorus; and entering the room he perceived the parish priest devoutly praying at the bed-side, his eyes closed, and the materials used in the last rituals for the dying standing beside him. Two candles were burning on the table close by, and by the feeble light which they emitted, mingling with the partial day-light that fell through the window curtains, he saw the pale, emaciated, and death-like countenance of his father, who lay stretched on the bed, while his own nurse, Bryan's mother, knelt beside, scarcely less ghastly, with dishevelled hair and streaming eyes.

The noise made by Cornelius in bursting into the room, and the exclamation which he could not suppress as he saw the deathly expression of his father's face, made the nurse and the priest both start from their places. When the old woman perceived him, she involuntarily ejacu lated his name, which was repeated by the priest in a tone of equal astonishment. At the sound of this dear-loved name, the father, on whom the hand of death had been just laid, but not with force enough to crush him, opened his languid eyes, cast a look around the room, recognized his son—and was restored by that glance to the existence which his followers had prematurely supposed extinct. He started up in his bed, and though unable to articulate, he opened wide his arms, and received the warm and tender embraces of his son, who felt as though he held to his breast a being arisen from the grave.

The effect of this momentary and miraculous scene was immense upon the astonished priest, —but to the feeble frame and superstitious mind of the poor nurse it was fatal. Her dreams of the preceding night, as worn out with watching she dozed by her master's bed, had all turned on Cornelius and her son; and dangers and death in a thousand shapes had flitted before her brain, which was prepared for such fancies by the scene of threatened dissolution which lay before her. Presentiments of the worst had afflicted her the whole morning; and as she watched the gradually decreasing light of her master's eyes, and saw the pallid hues of what she thought inevitable death stealing fast over his face, she gave up all hope, and had communicated to the anxious followers watching outside her belief that all was over. Prone to receive the intelligence of ill, the wild cry sounded the death of the revered sufferer, and the poor nurse thus confirmed in her fears, without being able to distinguish the truth that the one sprung from the other, had bowed her head in the long dreaded certainty. The appearance of Cornelius—his worn out and agitated look—the sudden starting up of his father—and, in short, the whole combination around her produced a shock, of violence sufficient to shake a firmer mind and stronger frame; and between grief, terror, and amazement, she sunk senseless on the floor.

The priest called aloud for help, and many of the people without hurried into the chamber. The greater part of these as rapidly retreated, on seeing what they believed the dead body of their master sitting upright in the embraces of Cornelius. A few, more resolute, following the directions of the priest, lifted the expiring nurse and bore her out into the air. Bryan, whose terrified anticipations had convinced him that his mother was dead, had been overjoyed at having his eager enquiries on his arrival answered so favorably as to his parent's state; yet his happiness was deeply dashed with sorrow at the news of his old master's death, which accompanied the glad tidings. He burst into tears, the ready expression of his mingled emotions, and was slowly preparing to mount the stairs, which his young master had so rapidly ascended, muttering prayers for the dead and blessings for the living, when he was met by some of the fast-retreating peasants, who, terrified and astonished, were incoherently exclaiming,

"He's alive! he's alive! The ould master is alive again—or his ghost's comed already to take master Cornelius away. He's alive, he's alive yet—or his spirit is there, one of the two."

Next came the body of the nurse, borne by a couple of sturdy peasants, and surrounded by the women.

"What's that you have there wid you?" cried Bryan with straining eyes as he recognized his dying mother.

"Who else would it be but Peggy Mulcahie, your own mother?" replied one of the men.

"What's the matter wid her?" falteringly asked Bryan.

"Nothing but a fright at seeing the master's ghost, or himself still alive—if it's him that's in it."

"She's dead, she's dead," cried Bryan; "let me near her, let me look at her:—she's dead, she's dead!"

"Och, it's only the fright," cried the surrounding group; all pressing close round the dying woman, and shutting out all chance of her recovery.

"It's no fright—it's death, I tell yiz all it's death that's on her," replied Bryan, in that tone of sorrowful energy which in an Irishman generally assumes the air of anger—"I knew she was to die—I saw her cross me three times on the road—and I heard her death-cry in the blast—I knew it, I knew it all, wirishthrew, wirishthrew!"

Bryan's prophetic exclamations carried their accomplishment with them. The listeners, convinced by the tokens which he reported himself to have had, that poor Peggy Mulcahie's fate was out of the reach of cure, gave her up as lost, and did not attempt any of those remedies which in such a case might have saved her. They stooped over her with stifling anxiety—shut out every breath of air—offered not the least relief—and saw the convulsions which terminated her life, without feeling the conviction that they might themselves be considered in a negative degree her murderers.

For several months after this day of arrival, Carmelino's father lingered on in that state of breathing animation which can scarcely be called existence, when a whisper of air might be thought sufficient to snap the fragile thread of life. Carmelino watched by his father's bed with incessant care, and ministered to him those assiduities which smooth the sloping descent to the grave. He gave his whole time to this sacred duty; but his attentions were the mechanical results of affection—for his mind was far away. He saw his father shrink and wither before his eyes, so silently and softly, that the palpable approach of death was not perceived—but the life of the sufferer seemed to fade away like the hues of a drooping flower. There was nothing in this state to rouse the positive energies of our hero's soul; and he appeared to himself as if partaking of that slumbering decay which fell across his father's tone and look, as the shades of evening sank upon the landscape which opened out before him. But his active thoughts were busily employed, fashioning into shapes of wildest fantasy those visions of imagined scenes which floated incessantly before him. She whom he adored was ever in prominent display, the passive inspiration of a world of moving wonders. In the heat of Cornelius's enthusiasm, numberless events were every moment springing into fancied existence, and all had reference to somewhat of her happiness and greatness. In all *he* was the leading actor—all was success and triumph, and delight—and while he thus cheated himself from the dark view of the destiny overhanging her and him, and brought her, as it were, within his mental grasp, the object of his real cares sunk almost unperceived from beneath his gaze, which looked widely into the futurity of an imagination that was more powerful than fact. When the event took place, and the last glimmering of life expired, and left him [illegible], [illegible] believe the evidence of [illegible]. [illegible] death, as he had heretofore seen it, was [illegible] the result of violence, and accompanied by [illegible] strugglings. He looked long on the [illegible] form that seemed quietly to [illegible] watching with intense interest for the signs which were to announce the spirit's flight from earth. We must not dwell on the anguish, which [illegible] was finished by the last pangs of death, as the tyrant set his stamp upon the brow of mortal clay; nor can we follow to the grave the sad procession, whose lamentations rung through the groves and valleys in a thousand echoes.

During the interval between Cornelius's arrival at home and his parent's death, Father O'[illegible] kept up a constant correspondence, narrating in his own peculiar way the events that were but imperfectly detailed in the public papers. The gloomy tone of the priest's communications had no ill effect on the enthusiastic hopes of his young friend, who considered the beauty, the courage, and the virtue of Marie Antoinette, a talismanic combination sufficient to render powerless the worst efforts of fate. Impressed with this deep-planted notion, he had no fears for her safety; but when his father's death dissolved the only tie which kept him from her service, he determined to return to it with a sole and effectual devotion. To attain this great object, he formed the resolution of selling every part of his small property in Ireland, with the exception of the venerated mansion where he and his ancestors had been born, and that gloomy spot in the lone burial-ground, where his father's body had been just laid to moulder with the ashes of his race. This proceeding was not one of immediate or easy completion. The forms of law required long delays, and the proceedings of lawyers did not shorten them. Purchasers enough were to be found, and competition ran high among those greedy sharks who fatten on the sacrifices of the imprudent, the generous, and the unfortunate.

Cornelius's property therefore sold well; and he remitted the whole amount of its produce to France, determined to embark his fortune with his life in the glorious hazard of giving freedom to the idol of his earthly worship. He weighed well the dangers he was about to encounter, not for his own sake, but for that of others, and he was resolved that none of those to whom he was so dear, and whom he was on the point of abandoning, perhaps, for ever, should have cause even to suspect his purpose; for he knew that the shock of an event which is irrevocable, produces much less misery than the preparatory pangs of anticipation. The sale was, therefore, secretly effected, and the faithful band of tenants and followers who had watched him from his cradle as their own and his house's hope, were passively transferred to the protection and service of new and unhonoured masters. This proceeding affected Cornelius's feelings, but did not move his resolution. It rather added firmness to his mind, which thus shook off the strongest of all shackles, in freeing itself from the association of old habits and early friends.

Cornelius saw the day arrive which was to separate him from his home, with the desperate intensity of resolution that wants but the echo of some old remembered thought to shake it into air. But he had wound his mind up to a pitch beyond the reach of recollections. Every feeling was concentrated and fixed, and he looked onwards towards his purpose with that unflinching exertion of the will which is the leading faculty of every resolute mind. Under pretence of a hurried journey for the arrangement of some affairs, he despatched a small packet of clothes and necessaries, by the speediest conveyance, to one of those provincial southern ports, from whence he had ascertained the sailing, on a certain day, of a vessel for France.

He mounted his horse and parted from Bryan, who held his stirrup unconscious of his purpose, with a sudden pang, that came nearer than any he had previously felt to the sensation which alone could decompose his projects. He clapped spurs to his horse, and only stopped him at the entrance of the desolate burying-ground, where he had still one spot of earth to call his own. He alighted, and tying his horse to a gate, which swung back on its creaking hinges as he touched it, he stept across the rudely formed graves, waded through the weeds and long grass which were matted together in the intervals between the mounds, and unheeding trod down many of the flowers, and white paper garlands planted by the sorrowing rustics, who were thus doomed on their next visit to the solemn spot, to many a superstitious pang at finding their simple offerings cast down and withered, by a touch which they, no doubt, deemed unearthly. Cornelius reached the little antique monument, which had been erected centuries before, and which was consecrated in his mind by all the natural feelings of family pride and love. There he knelt for a while; and invoking the shade of his late lost father, and letting his mind glance back one instant across ages of material facts, he seemed to mix in momentary communion with the shades of his ancient race, and swore, with uplifted hands and eyes, that he would perform some action worthy of their name and his. That short moment of unreal existence past, he returned into his actual self; and, with his every thought bent forward to his one great purpose, he hurried on his journey, and arrived in Paris, full of the swelling energy which leads to daring enterprise, to glory, or destruction.

CHAPTER XIII.

"WELL then, the blessing of Heaven be about you, for ever and ever, my darling boy! Then you're come back to me once more! Murther alive, but you're looking pale and thin! what has passed over you? And your eyes! By the powers they seem darting and burning in through me! And you're come! And your poor dear father, he's gone! The Lord receive him, and the Virgin, and Saint Patrick, and all the army of martyrs—for bad luck to the other that ever desarved to be with them better nor he. Oh, Cornalius, Cornalius, my darling, but I'm glad to clap my eyes on you again! but sorrow's the bit I can see of you now—for you're swimming and dancing in the big drops that's rising up between you and me. Sould all your fortune!—and kept the castle—and the monumint—and the grave in the ould burial ground!—and sent all the heaps of money over to Paaris in a letter! why then think o'that! O murther, murther, and it's yourself that's to the fore after all!"

Such was the greeting of Father O'Collogan, and his running commentary on his friend's appearance and conduct, when he received him into his open arms, at the office of the coach which carried him to Versailles. Cornelius replied by a cordial embrace; and he begged of the priest to inform him truly of those particulars of the queen's situation which he had only hastily learned as he passed through Paris. But this was not consistent with his companion's plan of conversational tact. He had a round-about way of coming to any point, and my readers know already that Ireland lay constantly in his road. On the present occasion, the recent arrival of Cornelius from that dear loved spot of so many recollections seemed to draw the good priest's feelings to it by a closer tie—and he could not resist the overflowings of his heart, which swept away for a time every thought connected with other topics. To Cornelius's anxious enquiries he replied, "Oh, botheration! my boy, don't be after talking to me about kings and queens and royal families—I can think of nothing at all, at all, but yourself and my darling country,—just for all the world like Ovid,—

Nescio quâ natale solum dulcedine cunctos
Ducit et immemores non sinit esse sui.- -

I know not how it is, not I,
That Ireland's always in my eye—
But somehow ever it my fate is
To think of bog and fog and grog,
Strong arms, warm hearts,
And mealy praties!

"Oh, thunder and fire, my jewel, let us talk about ould Erin! how is she getting on?—may be she's better—she can't be worse,—and you were '*here* the other day—Think o'that! why the ;ery smell of the turf's on the soles of your ;hoes! and you've sowld all, and quit her for :ver! but you'll go back to be buried, any how, or you wouldn't have kept the monumint. Oh ny poor country! that's the way every thing good forsakes you—and the divil a bad thing 'an live in it, barring its Englefied traitors,—not is much as a snake. *Nullus hic anguis, nec venenatum quicquam*, says ould Camden, no hanks to him for the same, the Sassanach!

Nothing venomous lives in the land, by the mass,
And 'tis there that you'll ne'er find a snake in the grass.

But she breeds plenty of human vipers to sting he mother that bore them, God knows! and Bede, what does the venerable Bede say?

"*Nullus ibi serpens vivere valeat*—"

Let a sarpent smell the soil—no more—
And he'll die without even touching the shore.

I wonder how the divil Strongbow and King

William and the likes of them, got landed, bad luck to them! but there's no use in talking—a day will come!"

And with this prophecy, fiercely announced, Father O'Collogan relapsed into the state of angry meditation which the mention of Ireland and the memory of her wrongs were always sure to create; so certainly indeed, that one might have supposed he only indulged in the subject for the sake of putting himself into a passion.

Cornelius, who knew his ways, contrived to soothe him by degrees, and soon softened the asperities of his temper and brought fresh tears into his eyes, by some touching details of his father's remembrance of him; by a mention of poor Bryan's loss and subsequent grief; and finally by the aid of that very bottle of native whiskey, of which I partook, as the reader may remember, some twenty years later, on the day of my first meeting with the worthy priest.

Our hero soon made himself master of every subject of information connected with the queen, and very speedily made known to her, through the former channel of his communications, that he had returned with life and fortune dedicated to her use. We must not stop to trace the many trials which put his fidelity to the proof, nor the various frustrated plans for relief to the royal sufferers, in which Cornelius was an actor. No want of money being experienced by them, his funds remained untouched and secure, and he lived with the greatest frugality; holding his property, as a sacred trust, for some urgent circumstance of want, which he now began to foresee hung over the king and queen.

When he arrived this second time in France, the year 1791 was far advanced, and many of those hurrying events had taken place which brought the royal family so quickly down the rapid gradations of their ruin—the first Federation of July 1790, when half a million of spectators ran riot in the confusion of what they called loyalty and patriotism, but which was, in fact, but the remains of servile adoration to the name of "King," mixed with an ignorant enthusiasm for that of "Country"—the revolt of the guards in the spring following, when Louis was stopped on his attempted departure for Saint Cloud, and his extensive prison, of all France, changed for the limited confinement of the Tuileries—the flight to Varennes, in June 1791, the arrest of the King, and its consequent effects, of utter alienation on the people and total despair upon the queen; when, finding all the efforts of her courage futile, she gave herself up for awhile as abandoned by heaven as well as man, and her beautiful profusion of golden hair was in one day turned to silver white, by the usurping touch of grief, which snatched the transmuting wand from the loosened grasp of time:—and finally, among these epochs of misfortune, came, in September, 1791, the acceptance of the constitution by the king and the legislative assembly—which instead of a splendid union of power with liberty, was merely the mockery of a junction, which fore-ran the degradation of the one and the consequent abuse of the other.

The last of these events was hailed (as was usual with every act which assembled the multitude and gratified their vain-gloriousness) with acclamation, rejoicing, and the treacherous semblance of happiness. But it plunged the actors of conceded royalty into deep sorrow. It dispersed the calenture which had so long deceived the monarch, and he saw in reality the booming waves of ruin where he had heretofore imagined the vegetation of rational change.

The various events thus hastily sketched, were the grand acts of the political drama which was obvious to the whole world; but it must be left to the imagination to figure the hours of bitter agony endured by the unhappy personages who filled the parts of chief victims in the tragedy. Independently of the positive misery inflicted on the royal family, every evil that cruelty could heap on pride was accumulated to crush the spirit of the queen. She seemed to bear "a charmed life" against the attempts of her ferocious enemies—and their only chance of ridding themselves of her gallant opposition to their process of royal degradation, was to bow her down in the depths of humiliation. During the period of our hero's absence from France two avowed assassins were detected in designs against her life. One was executed, contrary to her wish, and the other suffered to escape through her intervention. Various attempts to poison her were frustrated by her faithful servants—but although she went constantly into public and rejected all persuasion to wear armour, (such as the king put on at the celebration of the anniversary of the Federation) there was a something of protection in her own high bearing, that, as on the sixth of October at Versailles, must have paralyzed the many arms that seemed nerved to do her harm. Indignities too gross for record here were heaped on her with unflinching brutality. Nothing, in short, was left undone, even in her most domestic hours, that could be wounding to a woman of a proud and delicate mind, and indicative of moral turpitude and grossness on the part of her persecutors..

Such was the effect of these private atrocities

upon the leaders of the revolution, which had already proved that a nation may buy even freedom at too high a price, that almost all who had capacity sufficient to distinguish its just boundaries, turned with remorse and pity towards the victims of their miscalculating enthusiasm.

The king, his conduct and opinions, were universally overlooked, but every mind was bent upon his unfortunate consort. Mirabeau, La Fayette, Dumourier and Barnave, were one and all impressed with the desire to save the monarchy and serve the queen. But they had destroyed their own power and could not acquire her confidence. One of her weaknesses was the deep disdain which confounded all the revolutionists together, and marked them all as objects of hatred and distrust. She listened to their proposals, but she rejected their advice, and doubted their sincerity—and thus threw away successively a hundred chances of relief.

During all these struggles of wretchedness the queen's mind was in a state of utter misery —but her temper was never ruffled, her courage not once cast down, nor her bodily health impaired. When one of her attendants, on an occasion of serious mental agitation, requested her to take some antispasmodic drops, she made that reply which must have arisen from deep feeling and deeper grief—"It is women who are *happy* whose nerves are subject to disease;" but still the workings of her mind wrought a change in her appearance as striking as that produced by ill health. The grief which whitened her hair did not leave her countenance untouched. Her features displayed its stamp: she grew thin; and her eyes, so perpetually overflowing with salt tears, become swollen and red.

Cornelius had been two or three days in Paris, vainly endeavouring to procure a sight of the queen, and was suffering intense anxiety in his disappointment, when an evening was fixed for the public appearing of the royal family at the Italian Opera. They had already appeared, since the acceptance of the Constitution, at the Theatre François and the French Opera, and were remarkably well received. It was therefore determined that they should frequently shew themselves to the people, and high hopes were entertained that the public mind might settle down into a state of rational loyalty.

Cornelius was one of the first who took his station in the pit of the Italian Opera on the night in question. The house was soon filled; and, punctual to the appointed hour, the king, the queen, and the princess Elizabeth with their attendants entered their box. Their reception was good, notwithstanding that many emigrations had greatly reduced the number of the nobility, and that the theatre was filled with an audience not composed of what was formerly considered the higher ranks. But a strong feeling existed just then in favour of the royal party in the better classes of the people, for the struggle between *them* and the vilest, which ended in the triumph of the latter, had not yet taken place.

Cornelius gazed for a long time on the only object which was visible for *him*, unconscious of the applauding shouts which hailed her appearance; and it was not till the performance was far advanced, that he regained the composure necessary for a just understanding of what was going forward. The opera was proceeding tranquilly, and was nearly finished, when one of the singers laid an unfortunate emphasis upon a line which contained the phrase "oh I love my mistress," and accompanying the expression by a gesture of profound respect, turned towards the queen's box. No sooner was the sound uttered than it became the signal for a desperate change in the unanimous tranquillity which reigned in the theatre. Many of the audience understood Italian, which was the language of the performance; while the translations of the piece, printed with the original and scattered through the house, put almost every one in possession of the sense of what was uttered. No sooner was the word *Mistress* pronounced than several persons started up in the pit, by a simultaneous, and it might have been supposed concerted movement, and exclaimed with violence, "No Mistress!" "No

Master!" "Liberty! Liberty!" These cries were instantly answered from the boxes by loud shouts of "*Vive le Roi!*" "*Vive la Reine!*" "*Vive à jamais la Reine!*" The uproar was at its height, the performance stopped; every one in the theatre rose in his place except she who was the unintentional cause of the tumult, and she sat with a calm and dignified look while all around her trembled with agitation or fear.

Cornelius had been hitherto passive, feeling, but not acting in the scene, when a man beside him in the pit made himself particularly conspicuous by his shouts of "Liberty!" "No Mistress!" which he uttered with a menacing gesture directed against the queen. Our hero's blood mounted high—he could no longer restrain himself—but raising his arm he felled the insulter to the ground. This was the first blow struck, but the contest immediately became general and fierce. The great majority of the pit were opposed to the queen's party, but several of these jumped down from the boxes, and they made up in courage their deficiency in number.

Cornelius easily defended himself against the ill directed attacks of his infuriated assailants; and while those who came to his rescue struggled with their opponents in the French style of riot, scratching their faces, kicking their legs, and tearing the unpowdered locks of the Jacobins, which flew with the royalist curls profusely through the air, our hero pursued with persevering vengeance the man who had first roused his indignation into action. He seized him by the throat with one hand, and dealt with the other repeated blows, which his victim used no manly effort to avoid; but he screamed hoarsely for mercy, and to Cornelius's great astonishment addressed him by his name. Our hero ceased his assaults upon this directly personal appeal, and could scarcely credit his senses when his beaten foe whispered him that he was his former associate Armand.

A few hurried words of recognition passed

between them, and Cornelius in his amazement agreed to follow Armand from the theatre; for the king and queen had retired during this alarming scene, and our hero was doubly anxious to see after her safety without the house, and to learn somewhat of the career of the altered and degraded being whom he accompanied. They made their way through the combatants, and as they entered the street they saw the royal carriages moving off at a quick pace, escorted by the national guards, and unobstructed by the mob, who had not yet heard the particulars of what had passed within.

As Cornelius stared at his companion he could scarcely reconcile himself to the belief that he saw before him the once gay, flashy, well-dressed aristocrat, whose lace and ruffles and perfumery had made him conspicuous among the vain and haughty courtiers of Versailles. He was now pale and haggard; his black hair hanging undressed upon his shoulders, his clothes of a vulgar pattern and fashion, and his whole person neglected and even dirty. Armand read our hero's thoughts; and as they stopped under a feebly lighted gateway, he abruptly said, "I know what passes in your mind, Cornelius—but you must not think of me; your own safety and the service of the unhappy queen call loudly for a prompt attention to yourself. You see me changed—every way but in one respect; I am still—can you believe me? still deeply attached to my former benefactress. Do not reply to me by reproach or remark, but know that though publicly her foe, I labour night and day to serve—or rather to save her."

"What then are you, unhappy man, under this infernal garb?" asked Cornelius.

"Alas, I know not what!"—answered Armand with a deep sigh: but recovering his assumed air of [illegible], he quickly added—"No, I am of no [illegible] station—I am but a *patriot*, I sacrifice and suffer all things for my country's good: [illegible], think not of me—your very life hangs on a hair. Your conduct in the theatre [illegible] your fate if you are discovered. [illegible] your blows fell upon me; but still without instant measures of safety you are lost. Your only chance is in trusting yourself to me."

Cornelius was struck with the force and truth of these observations. He reflected a moment on the hazard to which he was exposed, and he determined to avail himself of the proffered aid of Armand.

"Will you give yourself up to me for this one night?" asked the latter earnestly—"You have the choice between safety and destruction. Decide, will you?"

"I will—I do," answered Cornelius with firmness.

"You shall have no cause to repent," exclaimed Armand.—"Follow me, and do in all things as I do. You must be initiated into the ranks of the patriots—you must be one of us in seeming—your safety and her's depend on your conduct—think and act afterwards as you will."

"I shall not flinch from any trial," cried Cornelius—"embarked in the adventure, I will go through with it."

"Enough," said Armand, "you are saved.—Now for the meeting of the Illuminati!"

At the sound of this name Cornelius started and shrunk back. He had heard of their horrid orgies, and knew their desperate designs.

"You hesitate?" said Armand—"you need not fear, for I have gone through it all."

"Fear," cried Cornelius contemptuously—"lead on."

Armand took him by the arm, and they stepped quickly and silently on through the crowded streets, crossed the Place Louis XV., and the bridge, and soon gained the banks of the river.

END OF THE SECOND VOLUME.

LONDON:
J AND ARROWSMITH, JOHNSON'S COURT, FLEET-STREET.

* 9 7 8 1 5 2 7 6 7 2 9 5 6 *

WS - #0169 - 241125 - C0 - 229/152/18 - PB - 9781527672956 - Gloss Lamination